KEREEN GETTEN grew up in Jamaica, where she would climb fruit trees in the family garden and eat as much mango, guinep and pear as she could without being caught. She now lives in Birmingham with her family and writes stories about her childhood experiences. Her work has been shortlisted for the Waterstones Children's Book Prize, the Spark Award, the Warwickshire Junior Book Award and the Jhalak Children's & YA Prize. *When Life Gives You Mangoes* and *If You Read This* are also available from Pushkin Children's.

DI ISLAND CREW INVESTIGATES

The CASE of the LIGHTHOUSE INTRUDER

Kereen Getten

Illustrated by Leah Jacobs-Gordon

Pushkin Children's

Pushkin Press
Somerset House, Strand
London WC2R 1LA

Text © Kereen Getten 2023

Illustrations © Leah Jacobs-Gordon 2023

The Case of the Lighthouse Intruder was first
published by Pushkin Press in 2023

3 5 7 9 8 6 4 2

ISBN 13: 978-1-78269-390-1

Designed and typeset by Tetragon, London
Printed and bound by Clays Ltd, Elcograf S.p.A.

www.pushkinpress.com

The
CASE
of the
LIGHTHOUSE
INTRUDER

Chapter 1

Fayson Mayor, the twelve-year-old FBI agent, has been recruited yet again to save the world. It's getting exhausting, as she has only just stopped a major assassination plot against the King of England.

"I'm tired of fixing your mess," Fayson says down the phone to the FBI head of division. "I'm not a robot. I need time to be a normal person, just for a day."

My phone starts to ring for real, and I jump out of my make-believe game and check the number on the screen. I stare at it in disbelief before putting it to my ear and answering hesitantly.

"Hello?"

"Fayson! You have to come to our holiday house for October half term. It's on a spooky island!" my twin cousins tell me, through rushed voices. They always talk over each other like it's a race to see who can speak the fastest.

I haven't heard from them in at least a year, so I'm shocked they're calling now.

"Yeah, weird things happen, like ghosts and flashing lights and stuff," one of them says, while the other makes ghost sounds down the phone for effect.

I try to identify who is speaking, but it's hard to distinguish between their voices right now. When we were younger, I could just about tell them apart because Aaron was taller and Omar had a dimple. Over the phone they sound the same, and it's been so long since I've seen them in real life.

I've caught glances of their holiday photos over Mama's shoulder when she stalks their mother's social media page. She mumbles, "I suppose I better say something before dey accuse mi of being jealous," before commenting on their photo, typing *That's nice* with a laughing face that she thinks is a happy face.

"Not that one, Mama," I have to keep correcting her. She will pull a face and say, "But dat one mek me look like me a grimace and I don't want dem to know what I am actually thinking."

Mama and her brother, Uncle Edmond, haven't been close for a while, but I think that maybe it's because he is never in the country and Mama is always working.

Now the twins are on the phone telling me about some island where they have a holiday home. Their father, Uncle Edmond, is a hot-shot businessman and their mother, Aunty Desiree, is a lawyer. They've always lived rich. They have a big house in the city too, with maids, and used to invite me to stay with them in the holidays, until they started travelling abroad.

Now, out of the blue, they're asking me to come and spend the holidays with them. I'm surprised they still have my number, with all their new rich friends around the world.

"I can't. I don't have a passport," I tell them, because I don't trust them. All they've ever done is play tricks on me.

There's snorting down the phone.

"What she say?" Omar (I think) says from the other end. Aaron repeats what I've said and they both dissolve into hysterical laughter.

"I don't see what's so funny," I snap down the phone. "Not all of us have passports to travel the world!"

"You don't need a passport," Aaron says, still snorting. "It's off Portmore."

I frown. "In Jamaica?"

"Yes!" they both shout. I still don't believe or trust them, so I say I'll think about it, and also I want to get off the phone because I don't appreciate being laughed at. I have better things to do, like save the world.

"Your mother already said you can go," Omar says. Which catches me off guard; Mama hasn't said anything to me.

"I said I'll think about it," I snap, and end the call. I collapse on my bed and stare at the ceiling, thinking about what they've said. An island that's not Jamaica but part of Jamaica? It's probably filled with posh houses with servants and pools, just like the twins' house in the city. I would feel out of place there. I am so different from all that.

Mama and I live in a small apartment on the top floor of a two-storey building not far from her work at the hospital. Our apartment faces a busy road, but across from that road is the library, my second home, so things are not that bad.

Mama works long hours and Ms Lee, an old lady from the apartment below, is always here watching me until she gets home.

Sometimes Mama will get home for dinner, sometimes I am woken up to her thanking Ms Lee in a hushed voice. Sometimes there are days when I don't see her at all.

Tonight is one of those evenings when I haven't seen her, but I stay awake by reading one of the books I borrowed from the library, even though I've read it three times already. I turn the light off, so Ms Lee thinks I'm sleeping, and read under the covers using the torch from my phone.

It is well past eleven o'clock when I hear the key in the lock: the familiar sign that

Mama is home. There is a quiet exchange between her and Ms Lee. I feel a surge of excitement to hear her voice. Knowing she is home safe, and her comforting tone, usually send me to sleep.

This time I wait until I hear Ms Lee leave, then I open the door a crack and peer into the living room. As I do, Mama collapses into the green sofa with a sigh, dropping her handbag on the floor and starting to peel off her work shoes.

I pad barefooted into the room, and I am standing in front of her when she opens her eyes. She jumps when she sees me.

"Lawd have mercy!" she cries, with her hand pressed against her chest. "Fayson, what are you doing out here?"

"Mama, yuh tell the twins I must go and spend the October holidays with them?" I ask.

She takes a breath and looks at me. "You don't want to go?"

15

I shake my head adamantly. "I don't have anything in common with dem. They too rich and they play too much tricks on me. I don't like dem."

She stifles a smile and gets up, walking over to the open kitchen that is part of the living room.

"Well, first of all, I didn't tell them anything. They begged their mother to ask me." Mama switches on the kettle. She mumbles something under her breath about her brother getting someone else to do his work, but I barely catch it and she turns her back on me when she says it.

I look up at her. "Why dem do dat?"

She shrugs, reaching for a cup in the cupboard. "Maybe they miss you."

I know that's not true. Not with all their rich friends and travelling the world. If they miss anything about me, it's throwing spiders in my hair and putting

water in my bed to make me think I've
wet myself.

"But why did you tell them yes, when you
know I don't like them?"

She laughs. "Fayson, you don't like
nobody, and that's the problem."

I pull up a seat at the breakfast bar and
lean on it. "Why is that a problem?"

Her smile fades. "Because ever since Lizzy
left, you don't talk to nobody. And you need
friends."

A picture of Lizzy, my best friend, flickers
through my head. We did everything together,
until she moved to Kingston with her family.
Now it's just me saving the world alone.

"I have friends," I tell her, and I start to
reel off the characters
in my latest book:

Hazley the
detective and her
dog Barnaby, who is

always by her side and may as well be by my side because he feels like my dog too.

It isn't until I mention the robot Herbert that she realizes what I'm talking about, and the hope in her eyes diminishes like I just told her she won a million dollars and then took it away.

She pours herself some camomile tea, because it helps her sleep. "Real friends," she says, glancing up at me, "not pretend ones."

"They're real to me," I say, feeling offended.

She shakes her head. "It's either spend half term with the boys or go to church camp again—if they let you in." Mama throws me a disapproving look.

I lower my eyes, remembering how I asked so many questions at the camp—like where in the sky God was, if they had a map they could show me, and why astronauts haven't found him yet—that they called me 'disruptive' and told Mama to come pick me up.

She looks at me gravely. "We lucky to get any of these opportunities, Fayson. You can't keep sabotaging them, because I don't have no money to pay somebody to look after you."

"We can go somewhere," I suggest. "You and me."

"I have no money to go nowhere," she says tiredly.

"Or we can go to the beach and get ice cream?"

"Which part of 'I don't have no money' you not getting?" she snaps.

My heart sinks, and the room becomes heavy with silence.

Mama's shoulders fall and so does her head. "Look," she says in a strained voice. "I would love to do all dem things with you, but I need to work. I can't afford to stop working, so this is what we have—church camp or your cousins. You need to pick one, or I will pick one for you."

Through the dim light of the street lamp shining into my room, I lie in my bed thinking hard about what Mama said. I think about how she works long shifts, six days a week, with only one day off and that day is busy with running errands. I think about how I follow her around to the bank and the supermarket, to the doctors and the hair shop, on that one day, because it's the only time I have with her.

I think about how we stop off at the patty shop and get my favourite coco bread and patty with fruit-punch box juice. Then sit outside on those iron chairs that are not very comfortable and watch people go by under the harsh heat of the afternoon sun.

I think about how quickly that day always goes and how, before I know it, it's night-time and Mama is getting ready for work again. I think about how tired she suddenly looks when she is ironing her uniform and how much it hurts knowing we won't get this time again for another week.

That's what I hate about church camp. They take us so far into the Blue Mountains that I don't even get that one day with her. I don't see or speak to her for three whole weeks, except for one phone call.

I think about the strict rules the camp has on not contacting home too much, early bedtimes, and annoying group activities that make me want to vomit.

I roll over on to my side and reach for my phone. I dial the last number, knowing Mama only gave me enough credit to call her in an emergency, so I hope this call isn't a waste.

"Yo," Aaron answers on the other end. "What time is it?"

"I'll come," I tell him. I can hear him rustling around.

"Really?" he says excitedly, and I can just picture all the pranks he's coming up with in his head right now.

"On one condition…"

"Okay, what is it?"

"You give my mother a job, on your island, for half term."

There is silence on the other end.

"You hear me?" I demand.

"How am I supposed to give your mother a job?" he asks. "I don't own the island."

"Talk to your parents, or your friends' parents, or whoever. But I'm not coming without her. Got it?"

I hear a sigh down the phone. "Okay," he says, "I'll talk to my parents."

I nod. "Good, then I'll come."

Chapter 2

When I enter the living room for breakfast, Mama is rushing around as usual—but this time she seems more irritable.

"Sit down and eat your food before it gets cold," she says, and turns her back on me to pack her lunch of corn beef and rice. I slide into the seat at the table feeling like I have done something wrong but not knowing what. She packs her lunch in her bag and makes her way over, sitting down across from me.

We eat in silence as the TV plays the news in the background. Outside, the road is already busy and cars whizz past beeping their horns at each other. There is a palm tree in our parking lot that is so tall I can see it framed by the window, its leaves swaying slightly under the morning breeze.

"Mama, did I do something wrong?" I ask eventually, unable to take the silence any more.

"You didn't do anything wrong," she says, without looking up from her tea. Then, as if she changes her mind, she places the cup down and glares at me. "Why you think I need you to find me a job?"

I look at her, confused.

"And with my brother!" she says, shaking her head. "You think I want to beg a job from my brother?" Then it clicks: my conversation with Aaron last night.

"I really wanted us to spend October half term together," I try to explain.

She shakes her head. "How many times, Fayson? I need to work."

"But if you work on the island, we can see each other," I tell her. "We can see each other every day, and because it's family, they might not even make you really work—just, like, sweep the floor or something but still pay you."

Mama looks at me quietly, her eyebrows wrinkled. She shakes her head slowly. I don't know what I've said now to make her sad, and I try desperately to think of what I could have said wrong.

"You think I should sweep my brother's floors?" she asks quietly.

My mind races. Is that wrong? Should I apologize? I don't want her to be mad at me, in case she sends me to church camp instead.

"You think I should give up my job as a nurse to sweep my brother's floors?" she repeats.

My heart falls into the pit of my stomach. I didn't mean that. I didn't mean she should only sweep floors. I go to tell her that's not what I meant, that all I wanted was for us to be together, when there is a knock on the door.

She pushes her chair back and walks across the tiled floor to open it. Ms Lee is on the other side.

"Good morning," she says cheerily.

Ms Lee is a retired teacher. She runs a group that is always organizing town meetings and baking cakes for the 'less fortunate'. She always tries to get Mama to join her group. Every day Mama promises her she will, but she never does.

Mama steps to one side, forcing a smile. "Good morning, Joanne. Come in," she says with a tired voice.

Ms Lee steps into the apartment with her usual big woven bag that will be filled with food even though Mama keeps telling her we don't need food, we have enough.

But we don't. We never have enough.

Mama disappears into her room while Ms Lee enters the kitchen and starts to unpack her bag, showing me everything she has brought. "And your favourite," she says, showing me a bag of tamarind balls. Normally that would excite me, but all I can think about is Mama being upset with me. I get up from the table and walk over to her bedroom, where I listen with my ear against the door to see if I made her cry. I can't hear any crying, so I knock gently.

"Come in."

I open the door and Mama is sitting on the edge of the bed, in front of her long mirror, taking the rollers out of her hair. She looks at me through the mirror.

"What is it, Fayson?"

I slide against the wall by the door with my hands behind me. "I will go to the island with my cousins," I tell her, even though my heart is heavy. I stare at my feet, so she doesn't see how sad it is making me to say it. "I will go by myself."

When she doesn't answer, I look up. She brushes her hair, then grabs her bag and heads to the door. She stops as she reaches me and kisses me on the forehead.

"Good," Mama says, "I'll tell them you're coming." She walks by me, then stops and lays a hand on my shoulder. "From what I hear, you won't even want to come back."

Then she is gone.

I listen as she tells Ms Lee goodbye and thanks her again for watching me. I hear the door open, then it closes, and I wish it wasn't like this. I wish Mama was as rich as her brother and we had an island we could go to.

Just me and her.

I wish good things happened to us the way they happen to my cousins all the time. I wish I had all the wishes in the world, and they would come true.

A week later I sit on the balcony outside our apartment, waiting for the twins to come and pick me up. They are due any minute now but Ms Lee has sent me outside so she can clean the floors. The front door of the apartment is open, and she is playing some old-time music and humming along to it.

My legs swing over the side as I watch Barry, who lives downstairs, riding his bike around the car park. I imagine he is an enemy spy, undercover, trying to catch me and expose me, just like in one of my favourite books: *Hazley and Barnaby Infiltrate a Spy Ring*.

He weaves in and out of the parked cars, shouting commentary to himself like he's one of those sportspeople on TV. Swinging off his hip is a catapult, and it suddenly gives me an idea. I could use it to protect myself from whatever tricks the twins are planning! All I would need is something to put in it.

"Barry!" I shout down to him. He spins his bike round sharply and comes to an abrupt stop. He squints up at me.

"Lend me your catapult," I yell.

He looks down at the catapult hanging off his belt. "This?" he says.

I nod. "Only for a few weeks. I'll bring it back."

He stands on his bike and spins round, shaking his head. "No."

I glare at him as he continues riding. "Why not?" I demand.

He glances back at me. "Because I don't want to give you nothing," he shouts up, "with your dry foot!"

I look down at my bare foot then at him angrily. "My foot is not dry, it's shiner than your teeth and your forehead!"

He swings his bike round. "Your foot so dry I can write my homework on it," he shouts, and laughs at his own joke.

I pretend to answer a phone, placing it to my ear. "Hello? Yes, hold on." I look down at Barry, who is eyeing me suspiciously. "It's for you. Old man Derek called, he wants his bike back."

He stops his bike, placing his foot on the ground. Then he unpins the catapult. "You can have it if you play with me."

I sigh, glancing over my shoulder at the clock in our flat. The twins will be here soon, and I need that catapult. It's the only defence I have against them and whatever they're planning for me. I slide on my shoes and walk along the long balcony and down the steps to the car park, but by the time I get there Barry is no longer alone but surrounded by four other friends also on bikes. I sigh again, annoyed with myself for falling for it.

Barry holds the catapult out in front of him. "If you catch it, you can have it." He spins his bike round and starts pedalling fast. I roll my eyes. Normally I wouldn't even entertain this, I would tell him to keep his rubbish catapult, but I need it. So I start running, knowing he's going to have to turn when he reaches the end of the car park.

One of his friends shouts, "Here," as he whizzes by me.

Barry throws him the catapult and the boy, who I recognize from school, catches it with one hand while steering his bike with the other. As I get close to one, they throw it to another, back and forth. I'm about to give up and tell them to keep it when they suddenly stop. All four of them look behind me, their mouths wide open.

Wheezing from running so much, I turn to see what they're looking at. A black SUV pulls into the apartment block. The twins are here.

"Jeez and peas," one of them gasps. "A prime minister, dat?"

I turn to look at him with a smug grin on my face. "They're here for me," I tell the group. "I'm being taken to a private island for the October holidays."

I watch their faces as they stare at me in disbelief. Barry clicks his tongue. "A lie. She don't know nobody."

"Fayson!" Omar sticks his head out of the window and waves to me.

I turn back to Barry with raised eyebrows and a smug grin, then I snatch the catapult out of his hand. "That's mine."

As I spin on my heels and bounce over to my cousins, I stick the catapult in the back of my jeans before they can see it.

"You be good," Mama says through the open door of the car. She has dashed out of work to see me off but we only had a few minutes. Uncle Edmond is packing my suitcase into the back. Aunty Desiree turns round in the passenger seat.

"She'll be good, Gee," she tells Mama, calling her by her nickname. Mama nods her head without looking at my aunt, and kisses me on the forehead.

"Call me when you get in," she says. "I've put enough credit on your phone."

"She can call from the house phone," Aunty Desiree says, smiling.

Mama nods again and pulls away as Uncle Edmond gets into the driving seat. She shuts my door and whispers, "Be good," again through the window, and I promise her I will.

As the car pulls out of the apartment block, I look out the back window, waving to her, but she only stands there until we turn on to the main road, then Mama is out of sight.

"Goodbye, Mummy... Kissy, kissy," Omar says from the other side of the car. He wraps his arms round his name-brand T-shirt, kissing the air. I feel in my back pocket for the catapult and wonder if it's too early to use it now. Then I realize I have nothing to use it with. All I have is a catapult but nothing to put in it yet

Good job, Fayson! I slump into the leather seat. *You're supposed to be an FBI agent and you can't even manage a catapult!*

Aaron is sitting behind us, playing a game with headphones on, and hasn't looked up once. Aunty Desiree looks round in her seat and smiles at me. It's been so long since I saw them, they all look so different. Even Omar, who's still pretending to kiss the air.

"It's so good to see you, Fayson," she says. Her face is full of makeup and her hair is a short pixie cut that is always straight. "It's been so long, hasn't it, Edmond?" She looks to Uncle Edmond, who glances at me in his mirror.

"Too long," he shouts. "You've grown so big, Fayson. You as big as your mother yet?"

I shake my head. "No, not yet."

He laughs like I've said something funny, and his eyes return to the road. "I forget how strong your accent is," he says. "We'll soon have you speaking English, don't worry."

I'm confused. What's wrong with my accent? I know I talk Patwah to strangers when I'm upset. I can't help it, it just comes out. But when I'm around people like Uncle

Edmond, I always make sure to speak my best English. That's what they teach us at school. But now he's telling me even my best English isn't good enough.

I clench my jaw, glaring out the window as everything familiar, everything I know, passes us by.

Aunty Desiree elbows him, and they start talking in lowered voices about how I should speak, with my uncle saying it's good for me to learn 'proper English'. I stare out of the window as the car speeds along the empty road out of town, wishing Mama was here with me.

Chapter 3

I wake to find Aaron standing outside the car staring at me. I reach for my catapult.

"Wake up," he says. "We're getting on the boat."

I rub my eyes and step out, looking around me. Uncle Edmond has parked his car in an empty car park. Aunty Desiree and Omar are heading towards a jetty, with a man carrying their luggage in a large cart.

"You coming?" Aaron says. I nod and run to catch up with him. He rests his headphones on his shoulders. "It's been a while since I've seen you," he says, tucking his game into his backpack and throwing it over his shoulder, which makes me flinch. I can never relax around these two.

He looks at me weirdly, then shakes it away as if he imagined something.

"You're tall now," he says. "I thought you would still be this high." He hovers his hand three feet off the ground.

I flash him a smile. "Because you still are?" I keep looking around me, wondering where we are.

Aaron chuckles. "You're still funny then."

I nod. There is a road behind the car park that I assume is where we came in. On the other side of that road are pink and white houses that look like holiday homes. In front of us and slightly to the right is a white building, where Uncle Edmond emerges with a man wearing a white shirt and white trousers. They are deep in conversation and follow Aunty Desiree towards a jetty directly ahead of us that leads to a small white boat rocking gently in the sea.

"Where are we?" I ask Aaron, noticing Omar jump on a boat ahead of his mother.

"Portmore," he replies, pointing ahead. "That boat, the one Omar is on? Will take us to Lighthouse Island."

I don't want to tell him I thought we were driving there, even though he had already told me it was separate from where we live. I nod as though I knew all along and realize that this is probably going to be my act for the rest of the holiday: pretending I know things that I don't.

I already feel out of place, and we haven't even got there yet.

At the end of the jetty, we all climb on to a small white boat with a cloth over the top to shade us from the sun. There are long white benches on either side and our bags are laid in the middle of the floor. Uncle Edmond helps me on and asks me if I had a good sleep. I tell him yes thanks, I did.

"Yes, *thank you*," he corrects me, with that same smile. "Not 'yas tanks'."

I frown, because I'm sure that's what I said... but Mama doesn't want me to be any trouble, so I repeat it exactly how he did, and my uncle seems pleased.

He doesn't seem to realize how bad he's made me feel. When he sits next to Aunty Desiree on one bench, I purposely sit on the other side, because I'm beginning to remember that there was something I didn't like about Uncle Edmond and his wife.

Unfortunately for me, sitting away from him means I am forced to sit in between Aaron and Omar, which is just as bad but in a different way.

The man in the white shirt and trousers starts the engine, and it's loud as it pulls away from the dock. I hold on to my smaller bag, which has all my books, my phone and my diary in it. The water bellows under us as the boat bounces over the waves like those bumpy water park rides that make you seasick.

I've only ever been in a boat once. It was on my birthday and Mama surprised me with a boat ride to see dolphins. But I was so sick, I only saw the choppy waves lunging at me as I threw up over the side.

I can feel my stomach churning now, so I close my eyes to try and block it out. The last thing I want to do is throw up on Uncle Edmond's boat. He would not be happy, and neither would Mama, so I squeeze my eyes as tight as I can and beg the boat to hurry and reach land.

Aaron nudges me and says something, but I can't hear over the engine or the waves. He looks worried. I'm too nauseous to find out why.

Eventually, the boat slows and the engine quietens. Aaron tells me to open my eyes and look. So I do, cautiously. We have reached Lighthouse Island. He points over his left shoulder to another dock, which is getting closer. Beyond the dock are rows of white golf carts, all parked in a line, and beyond that are large houses dotted around the island, all set among trees, some on a small incline.

The boat pulls up to the jetty and a man on the dock, who Uncle Edmond calls Thompson, grabs a rope thrown to him. He ties it round a wooden pole. The engine is off, but the boat is still rocking and so is my stomach. I need to get off this boat as quickly as possible and feel dry land.

Everyone starts to climb off the boat one by one, helped by Thompson, but they seem to be taking their time and my stomach is still riding the last wave we were on. I wait behind Aaron, trying not to think about the gurgling of my insides, when I feel myself being pushed overboard, then pulled right back. I turn in horror to see Omar laughing hysterically.

"Your face!" he hollers. "You really thought I was going to push you in the sea?" My stomach growls and my head spins, then before I have chance to respond, I empty my breakfast all over his fancy T-shirt.

Even after his mother wipes him down with some wet wipes, Omar is still moaning when we reach the golf carts I spotted from the water. I hold my stomach, hoping nothing else comes up.

"Who wants to go with who?" Uncle Edmond says, standing between the two carts.

"I'm not going with her," Omar moans, glaring at me. He gets into the cart on the left, folding his arms against his chest, then realizes his shirt is wet and moans again.

If I wasn't feeling so sick, this would feel like a win.

Uncle Edmond points me to the other cart. "Me and you in this one then, Fayson?" I would rather not ride with him, but there doesn't seem to be a choice.

"I'll ride with you too," Aaron says, slipping in beside me on the back seat, which faces the opposite way to the steering wheel. The cart pulls away with Uncle Edmond at the wheel, and behind us Aunty Desiree follows with a pouting Omar and our bags.

The carts travel up a smooth gravelled road with no other vehicles on it except us. Well-kept grass flows on either side, occasionally interrupted by a stone wall with a house behind a long driveway. The roads are clean. Pink, red and white roses decorate the edges of each house.

The island is quiet, except for the noise of the cart. Aaron plays music from his phone, bopping his head along, occasionally making faces at his brother. Omar ignores him, staring at the passing houses with a scowl on his face. A few minutes later we turn off to the left down a long curved driveway only passable by one car. Neat grass and more pink and white flowers layer the sides, with the occasional towering tree to break them up.

The drive opens into an entrance with a grey iron fountain in the middle and a large one-storey house with brown-tiled roof. I don't know why I'm surprised how grand it is. I should know by now they only do things big. Uncle Edmond drives round the fountain and stops outside wide stone steps that lead to wooden double doors.

Aaron jumps off and I follow, trying
to keep my face as neutral as possible, as
though I go to houses like this every day.
Inside, I'm super aware that I am suddenly
in a completely new world. I feel eight years
old again: when Mama would drop me off
at their house in the city for the summer
and I would feel so out of place. Like I didn't
belong.

This is a world away from my apartment
in the city and I feel homesick already.
I wonder what Mama is doing and if she
misses me like I miss her.

A woman wearing a light-blue uniform with a white apron appears from inside and welcomes the family with open arms.

"Mr Edmond, Mrs Desiree, I got all the beds ready and there is lunch waiting." I follow Uncle Edmond inside the house and into a foyer with high ceilings and corridors either side. The foyer leads down three steps into a lower living room, filled with large cream sofas facing each other and a glass table with oak legs in the middle. Cream chests of drawers with wood tops fill the walls on either side of the living room and a large TV hangs from the wall.

"And for Fayson too?" Aunty asks, as Uncle Edmond disappears round the corner.

The woman turns and glances over at me. She smiles warmly. "Of course," she says. "Everything is ready for her, just as you asked."

Aunty Desiree beckons me forward. "Elma will show you to your room, and the boys will show you the rest of the house later. Right, boys?"

"Hmm," Aaron mumbles, back on his phone. Omar storms past me and down into the living room, disappearing to the right behind his father. Two smaller matching chairs are placed next to the sofas facing towards us, and behind are floor-to-ceiling glass doors pushed back into the wall revealing large stone pots and a wide veranda with outside tables and chairs. As we walk through, I can see a large garden that slopes downwards to a pool and a clear view of the sea.

I think about Mama and what she must be doing. How she will come home to an empty house. I wince as I think about her being alone, without me. How she doesn't have a nice window to look out from, or a garden to sit in when she wants to relax. Thinking about her makes my chest ache as though someone is hitting me from the inside.

We walk through the living room and I'm careful not to touch anything, in case I break something and Uncle Edmond makes me pay for it. On the other side of the room, we turn right down a long corridor where there are more rooms with big, heavy wooden doors. It is at one of these rooms that Elma stops and opens the door. Further ahead I see Aaron opening a room to the left and disappearing inside.

Inside, the room is surprisingly darker than the rest of the house, with a large oak bed against the wall, floor-to-ceiling built-in shutter wardrobes, all dark wood, and further to the left of the door what looks like a bathroom. I crane my neck to look in awe. I've never had my own bathroom before! Elma hurries across the room and pulls back the curtains to reveal doors that lead out on to a patio and the garden.

"This is all for me?" I whisper, walking around the room in disbelief. Elma laughs, patting down the bed even though the bed is tidy.

"It's all yours. There are towels in the wardrobe." She walks round me and over to the door. "When you're ready, come back into the living room. There's lunch waiting for you." I nod and she closes the door.

I stand in the middle of the room taking it all in, before going over to the bed that seems to have at least three mattresses it's so high. I jump on it and collapse, with my arms and legs spreadeagled, glad to be on dry ground again. Even if this ground is nothing like what I'm used to.

I think about Fayson FBI, and how this would be her kind of house, because she's super famous and good at her job, so that

51

would mean she would be rich too. I imagine how this island would be a perfect escape from saving the world, but also a perfect place for my enemies to find me. Islands are the best places to have a fight-off with the enemy. They can sneak up on you without you knowing, but also you can get rid of the bad guy, throw them in the sea and no one would find them. Just like in *Hazley and Barnaby: The Cursed Island*.

I start to daydream about a small boat arriving, and my enemies slipping on to the far side of Lighthouse Island, dressed all in black, and creeping to my house. I slice the air with my hand, practising all the moves I have been taught from the best fighters in the world.

I hear a sudden noise and sit up. I listen. There it is again. It sounds like someone outside my door. I've been expecting the boys to pull something, but I didn't think they would try so soon. I slide off the bed and creep over to the door. I stand to the side, so that when it opens it will hide me.

I slip the catapult out of my pocket, only to remember I still have nothing to put in it. I press my back against the wall, trying to think of what I can do with a catapult that has nothing to fire. Maybe hit them over the head with it? That might sting but it won't stop them. Plus, Omar the big crybaby would run to Uncle Edmond, and Uncle Edmond might call Mama and tell her I'm not behaving. I slip the catapult back in my pocket, sighing that after all my effort to get it, now it's useless.

While I wait behind the door, I decide I will at least have the element of surprise and can stop their plan with that. So, I wait. Nothing happens. The door handle doesn't turn. No one comes barging in. I am beginning to think I may have imagined the noise, when I am grabbed from behind and a pair of sweaty hands covers my eyes. I start kicking and thrashing.

"Fayson Bailey, you have been summoned by the Greatest Gang of All Time."

I stop kicking. "The what?"

"The greatest gang," Omar says irritably. "Let's go."

Chapter 4

Through the gaps of his fingers, I can see the marble floor as Omar leads me clumsily outside into the backyard through the sun doors. They take me down some steps, Aaron leading, and I catch glimpses of a large rectangular pool to our left, with grey paving around it and a few white tables and matching chairs.

"Why do you have to cover my eyes?" I demand, almost missing a step.

"Because the meeting is secret," Omar says, and his brother nods in front of him.

"If you don't get into the club, then you won't know where we meet, will you?"

I can't tell if he's joking or being serious, and almost tell them that I can see through his fingers but change my mind in case I need to escape.

We take five steps down to the bottom of the sloping garden, and then to the right, on to the grass. We stumble along a small path with triangle-paved stepping stones and stop in front of a small wooden hut stood against perfectly cut bushes.

Through Omar's fingers I see his brother knock on the wooden door in a series of knocks that is obviously meant to be a code for entry. It's straight out of a secret agent book, which surprises me because I have never seen the twins read.

There is a noise from the inside that sounds like the door being unlocked, but the person on the other side seems to have some trouble opening it as they twist the handle one way, then the other.

Aaron sighs. "Just pull it," he hisses.

"I am," a girl's voice says on the other side. They're rattling the door. Aaron pushes from the outside and finally it's flung open. A girl looks out at us, flustered. "Got it," she announces proudly.

Aaron shakes his head at her then nods to me and the girl's eyes fall on me, her hand clasping her mouth like she said something she shouldn't have.

For an awkward minute no one moves. Then, "Oh, sorry!" she cries with a nervous giggle, and the girl steps aside, allowing Omar to lead me in.

Inside the hut, I can make out a few other people and a desk at the front with another girl behind it. Everyone is looking at me as I am shuffled to the middle of the room by Omar.

"You can let her go," says the girl behind the desk, and to my relief Omar's hands drop. I wipe my face with the back of my hand, then look around me, taking it all in.

It's a small hut, not very wide, with just enough room for three or four kids to move around freely. But there are—I glance round the room at their faces—at least six of us here. They've managed to get a desk in, and some beanbags. There is a framed group motto on the wall behind the girl at the desk that reads, *Never speak of the hut, outside of the hut.* Which doesn't seem like a good motto at all. But it's a nice little setup.

"So, this is her?" the girl says, looking me over. I guess she must be the boss of whatever this is, because she's the only one with a seat and a desk.

Omar nods proudly. "She reads lots of books, so she's super smart," he says. His brother gives him a look.

"This is our cousin, the one we told you about," Aaron says, pointing at me just in case they didn't know who he was talking about. "She's top of her class in everything, and nothing gets past her. She's really good at figuring things out."

I glance at him, feeling surprised. I've never heard either of the twins talk about me like this. I thought they hated me.

"Yeah, she would always figure out our tricks," Omar adds. Everyone turns to me again and I can feel them looking me over. I feel strange, like I want to smooth down my hair and check my top isn't inside out.

"What's your name?" the girl behind the desk asks. My eyes fall on her, about the same age as me, maybe a few months older. She's tall, like, basketball tall. She wears long thick twists down her back which she keeps flicking off her shoulder then pulling each twist back one at a time.

"Fayson," I answer, and my voice sounds croaky, so I clear my throat. "Fayson," I repeat, clearer this time. I try to remember that I am Fayson FBI who saves the world, to stop the nerves that are swirling around inside me. I don't know why I am nervous, they're only kids like me, but this seems like more than just making friends, which I'm not very good at anyway.

"Well, Fayson, we don't just let anyone into our gang. Why do you think we should let you in?"

I frown. "I didn't know anything about your gang until five minutes ago when they—" I point to my cousins—"kidnapped me."

"It wasn't a kidnap," Omar says, laughing nervously.

I look at him. "You broke into my room, covered my eyes and forced me out the house."

He laughs, shifting his feet. I turn back to the girl, whose eyes haven't left me.

"I don't know why I'm here, or what you want from me or what this is, so if you're not going to tell me, can I go? I'm tired and I've been sick." I shoot a look at Omar.

She stares at me for some seconds, and I'm thinking about leaving when she says, "You can stay."

She beckons for one of the boys to get me a seat. The boy, with a low cut and lines in his hair, moves the beanbags in a semi-circle, and one at the front. The girl gets up from her chair, comes round the desk and nods to everyone.

They all sit down so I copy them, sitting on a yellow beanbag.

The girl looks at me again. "We are the Greatest Gang of All Time."

"That's a really weird name for a gang," I say.

She glares at me. "It's got all our names in it. 'The' and 'Time' for Tia—that's me, I get two words. 'Greatest' for Gaby—" she points to the girl on my left, who opened the door. I can see now she has two long cornrows and braces.

"'Of' for Omar," Tia continues, nodding to my cousin, who is picking his nose in the corner, "and 'All' for Aaron and Ace." Lastly she nods to the boy who laid out the beanbags. Her lips pull in a smug smile.

I blink at Tia. "So who's the other G, for 'Gang'?"

She stares at me, and I feel a rumble around me as the others look away.

"'The Greatest Gang of All Time'?" I repeat slowly. "You're missing someone with the second G."

Her mouth pulls in a thin line. "We don't have anyone with another G."

"Then why didn't you choose another name?" I ask, baffled. "You know, with letters that actually work." I look around to see if I'm the only one who thinks this is the worst name in the entire universe, but no one will look at me and I'm starting to realize that Tia is not only the boss, but they seem to be afraid to tell her the name sucks.

"That's not why you're here," she says through clenched teeth.

"Then why am I here?" I ask.

"Your cousins say you can figure anything out."

I look over at my cousins, wondering why they're bigging me up so much when we've barely spoken in the last year. They give me

63

a hopeful nod, so I turn back to Tia. "Figure what out?"

Gaby leans forward, smiling with wide, excited eyes. "How good are you at solving mysteries?"

Chapter 5

My heart skips a beat. I think about all the mystery books I've read. How I always wanted to be a detective with my own case, finding clues and piecing them together. I think about Fayson FBI and how she's always wanted a real-life mystery.

"The best," I hear myself say, and straight away I wish I could take it back. Why would I say that? What was I thinking? The only real-life mystery I ever solved was finding my lost science book under the bed.

They all look at each other, smiling. "Told you," Omar says triumphantly.

"Good." Tia smiles for the first time, but I'm not sure it's genuine. "Because we have a big one. None of us has been able to figure it out."

I think how unsurprising that is considering they can't even figure out a good name for their group. "So, what is this mystery?"

Tia says we need to wait until it gets later in the day. "It only happens when it gets dark." I can tell she loves avoiding my question. "We can't tell you what it is yet... but you'll see."

I wonder what this mystery could be that only happens in the dark. It's frustrating to wait, and I feel a lingering nausea from earlier. Everyone settles down on the floor, gossiping about the 'thing' I am about to see.

We wait in the hut, and after ten minutes the chatter begins dying down. Then twenty, then thirty minutes pass. We become restless. Omar asks if he can go home and come back later.

"No," Tia snaps from her desk. There's a book laid out in front of her: *How to Be a Good Leader.* "If you leave, then you won't come back in time, and I don't want to chase after you, Omar."

"I would come back," he mumbles.

Tia returns her gaze to her book. "No you wouldn't," she replies. "Everyone knows you're unreliable."

Omar leans back against the wall, pulling his knees up to his chest with a heavy sigh. I watch as he sinks into the floor as though he's been told off by his parents. I look over at Aaron and notice he is also glancing at his brother, his eyebrows wrinkled, his mouth pulled to one side. Aaron catches me studying him and he looks away quickly, avoiding my eyes.

"Didn't your mama say she has food out for us?" I suggest to Aaron.

He glances at me, then at Tia. "Well, it was Elma, but yeah," he replies, "she did."

I nod firmly. "We can't leave her waiting. Adults get really annoyed about that kind of stuff." I stand up and head for the door. "I don't know about you, but I don't want to upset Uncle Edmond. Mama said one time he got so mad his eyes were bulging and him snarl like a snake!"

I open the door and let myself out. I am only a few steps up the path when I hear footsteps behind me. I stop and turn to see Omar running to catch up with me, then Aaron not far behind, followed hesitantly by Gaby and Ace.

"Good call about the food," Omar says, patting me on the back. I am about to continue up the path when Tia appears in the doorway.

"I didn't say any of you could leave the hut," she snaps. "I'm the leader. You can't leave unless I say so."

The group stops in their tracks and for a moment I think they might actually listen to her.

"We need to eat," I tell her firmly. "Aren't you hungry?"

Tia's mouth twists from side to side, then she steps out of the hut. "It could be a long night," she says tensely, "so I say we all get something to eat." She barges through the group and ahead of me. "Their maid always makes too much food anyway."

In the living room, sure enough the table is filled with sandwiches, cakes, potato chips, patties and coco bread.

Elma appears from the kitchen with a jug of juice, placing it on the table. She smiles at me gently. "Help yourself, Ms Fayson," she says before returning to the kitchen.

The others start piling their plates with food and talking about previous visits to the island. Tia walks round the table, turning her nose up at everything, eventually settling on a slice of coco bread with some cheese. She sits at the table but everyone else spreads out around the room: Omar on the recliner, Aaron and Ace beside each other on the sofa.

Gaby slides up to me with one of everything on her plate.

"The chicken pattie is the best," she suggests, as I stare at the table filled with food. When I don't answer, she puts one on my plate with a slice of coco bread, but all I can think about is how much food there is here. How many days Mama and I could spend feasting on all this. It would be like Christmas and our birthdays all at once! I feel a lump in my throat and my eyes mist over.

Gaby takes my arm and leads me over to the sofa opposite Ace and Aaron, who are in loud discussions about their last trip to Lighthouse Island.

"We had a storm," Gaby explains. "It was really bad. We all camped at Tia's house and told ghost stories." Gaby glances over at Tia, who doesn't seem to be paying us any mind. "But then she got too scared and asked us to leave." Her voice lowers. "We ran to Ace's house because it was closest and stayed there until the storm was over, but Tia got mad with us for leaving her out."

As if hearing her name, Tia looks up. Gaby takes a big bite of her sandwich.

"So, what were you doing in that storm, Fayson?" Aaron asks, turning the attention on me. "It was pretty bad all over the island."

I remember the storm well. Mama was stuck at work and couldn't get home. So it was me and Ms Lee, who spent most of the time holding on to me and telling me not to worry, when she seemed more worried than I did. Even when the electricity went out I wasn't scared. It was exciting. I imagined it was my enemies who had arrived to take me, that it was them, not the storm, that had cut the lights.

I feel all their eyes on me, waiting, even Tia. "It was boring." I shrug. "We waited it out in the living room."

Omar shakes his head dramatically. "That's the worst place to be! You're supposed to go where there's no windows."

"No, that's a tornado," Aaron argues. They go back and forth, with Ace chiming in.

Now the attention is off me, a breath of air that I didn't know I was holding escapes me. I think about my small apartment in the city, how we could fit two of it in this house, maybe three. I think about Mama and what she will be eating today while we feast on all this food.

I feel someone's eyes on me and turn my

head to see Tia watching me from the table. She doesn't smile. Doesn't say anything. Just stares, with a puzzled expression.

It's early evening when we return to the hut. Tia orders us all to sit down. I stay standing. She stands from behind her desk and for a few seconds we have a stare-off, her waiting for me to sit, me waiting for her to say something. At last she breaks the stare, turning to the rest of the group and clearing her throat to get everyone's attention.

"It's time," is all she says, but it's enough to stir up excitement in the room again. She walks round her desk and over to me. "This isn't something we can tell you. This is something you need to see for yourself." She leads me out the hut and back on the path.

This is what I've always wanted, to be a real-life detective. It is like someone has gone into my head and made my dreams come true. So why am I so nervous?

Chapter 6

The chatter continues along the path at the bottom of my cousins' garden, and round the house to the front where we arrived earlier today. Gaby tells me to stay off the grass because the twins' mother doesn't like it.

"Typical parents, you know?" she says as Tia eyes me from slightly further ahead. "They like making things perfect for other adults, but we can't touch any of it."

"You just can't touch anything because you break everything," Tia interjects as we reach the sweeping driveway.

Gaby lowers her eyes, clasping her hands in front of her. "That's not true," she mumbles.

Tia leads us along the driveway and out towards the main road of the island. "It is true, Gaby," she says without looking behind her. "I can touch whatever I want, because I'm not clumsy like you. I respect my parents' things, and so they trust me. That's how it works."

"Besides," she adds, "my father will do anything for me." She glances over at me. "When I was younger, he would play any game I wanted. He would say, 'What do you want me to be today?' But that was when he wasn't playing football overseas. He's a super famous football player."

"World Cup famous?" I ask, slightly interested. Mama liked to listen to the World Cup so she could cheer Jamaica on.

Tia rolls her eyes as though I've said something silly. "More famous than that."

I frown, wondering what could be more famous than the World Cup.

There are a lot of things that are making me curious about this group. Their name: who chose it? And why did they get together? Why these five? Are there more kids on Lighthouse Island or is this it? But what interests me most is Tia. Why is she the leader, and why does everyone seem to be afraid of her?

As we reach the end of the driveway, she turns left on to the one road that Omar says circles the island. Tia doesn't look behind her; she just expects us to follow.

I hear my name being called and turn to see Aaron catching up with me.

"So what do you think of the group?" he asks, and his eyes are earnest, as though my approval means everything.

I shrug. "I don't know much about everyone yet."

"You don't know the people," he says, "but what do you think about our group solving mysteries? It's cool, right?"

It is cool that my cousins come here every school holiday to do the one thing I dream about in my small bedroom back home.

"I need to see what you do first," I tell him, because I don't want him to think he's done me a favour by bringing me here.

Aaron nods. "Yeah, that seems fair."

We follow the road as it curves round the island to the right: houses peering through trees, more long driveways and nothing but silence.

I notice muddy footsteps all over the road, going in different directions, and ask him who's being walking in mud.

Aaron laughs. "That's Thompson, the island's caretaker. He walks round the island two or three times a day, and in the marshes too. Thompson thinks if he doesn't do his rounds every day, then someone might sneak on to the island and kill us all, and he will be to blame. He's weird like that."

The road comes to an end, and in front of us is nothing but green shrubs and rocks. We all stop at the edge in a line and look out at the scene before us. Beyond the shrubs and beyond the rocks in the distance is a lighthouse. I don't remember seeing it when we arrived earlier. Maybe it was too far on the other side and blocked by trees and houses. Or maybe I was too sick to notice anything around me.

"That," Aaron says, nodding ahead, "is where we're going."

I follow his gaze. The lighthouse sits in the middle of rugged rocks with bushes growing in between. My heart picks up pace as I stare wide-eyed at the looming tower.

This feels like something out of a movie, before the adventure begins. FBI Fayson's very own Lighthouse Island adventure! My eyes light up and I can barely contain my excitement.

The sun is starting to set as we follow Tia in a single line. There are birds flying above us, but no other sounds. It's eerily quiet on this island.

Beneath the plants and stones is a tiny path that has formed from the feet that have forced the ground flat. There is barely enough room for me to put one foot in front of the other.

We manoeuvre around the smaller rocks and the shrubbery in our way. In the distance, to the right, beyond the shrubs and the jagged rocks, the sea looks flat and calm and nothing like what it was when we were on the boat. From here you could mistake it for being asleep, but I know that is a trick to lure you down there.

Further off in the distance, some miles away, you can see the outline of the main island, where Mama is still working and will go home tonight to an empty apartment. I feel a pang of sadness and wish there was a way for her to be here too. It seems so unfair that she works every day and we still have nothing, while Omar and Aaron have all this, and I've never seen their parents work.

Tia stops suddenly, looking at the area around her. We have come to a flat piece of ground that looks as though it has been cleared. She finds a space and sits down. The others follow suit, trying to fit into the small space. Aaron pulls me down beside him.

We are squashed together like sardines on the ground. I pull my legs up to my chin just to fit into the tiny space. Large shrubs surround us, but through the gaps of the leaves you can see glimpses of the lighthouse.

"Now what?" I ask him.

Aaron puts his finger to his lips. "Now we wait," he whispers.

I raise my eyebrows at him, but he doesn't say anything else. The others fall silent too. I'm confused. What we are waiting for. A murderer? A kidnapper? A thief? What is it about the lighthouse they couldn't figure out that they need me?

"Anyone got any food?" Ace hisses, looking round the group. Everyone shakes their head. Ace groans. "We always forget food."

"*You* always forget food," Tia snaps. "You're the one who complains about it, so you bring it next time. Or don't you have any food in your house?"

Ace stares at the ground. "I have food," he mumbles.

Tia scoffs, "Oh yeah, I forgot your dad locks everything in your house so you can't steal anything!"

Ace glances in my direction but looks away quickly when we make eye contact. The group falls silent again, in the same way they did back at the hut.

I'm developing a real dislike for Tia. I really want to say something, to tell her to stop being so mean, but every time I think of speaking up I catch Aaron giving me those pleading eyes again, as though he knows what I'm thinking and he's begging me not to show them up.

"Here," Omar says, slipping a hand into his pocket. He pulls out a clear bag of sweets. "Lemon drops," he says, wiping his nose with the back of his hand then fishing the same hand into the bag and pulling out a sweet. He offers it to Ace, who turns his mouth up in disgust.

"I've changed my mind."

Omar shrugs. "More for me," he replies, and throws a sweet into his mouth.

Gaby crawls from where she is sitting and slides in next to me. "The lighthouse hasn't worked for years," she says. "Not since we moved here anyway."

I stare at the lighthouse, wondering what stories it has to tell from the past. Gaby wiggles even closer to me and she beams.

"I think we're going to be great friends," she says, nudging me. "Do you think you might like to be the leader some day? Not right now, and only if you like our group but you seem like you would be a fair leader." She glances in Tia's direction and cups her mouth, whispering, "I would vote for you, but don't tell Tia I said that."

Suddenly, as if out of nowhere, it becomes pitch black, and at the same time the group starts getting excited. Everyone moves around so they are facing the lighthouse. Aaron checks his phone.

"Thirty seconds," he whispers.

All eyes turn to the lighthouse and my heart starts beating fast. I feel Gaby's hand on my arm. "I don't like this bit," she murmurs. Tia tells her to be quiet.

Aaron starts to count down. "Ten... nine... eight... seven... six..."

Behind me, Tia tells me to keep an eye on the top of the lighthouse, where the window is. So I stare at it hard, my heart beating faster with every second, not knowing what to expect.

"Five... four... three... two... one."

Gaby squeezes my arm suddenly as a dark figure appears against the window and a light flashes out to sea.

"One… two… three," Tia counts the flashes behind me. "Now he'll put the light down."

The figure bends down and disappears, then stands up again.

"Now he waits."

The figure stands still for a minute or two, and then is gone.

"Who was that?" I ask no one in particular.

"We don't know," Tia says. "It's no one that stays here, we've checked. The person never leaves, and we never see them go in. But every night that happens."

I stare at her blankly. "It must be someone you know." This is a tiny island where everyone seems to know each other.

She shakes her head. "No one goes up there. The adults stay in their houses or by the beach. They never come to this side of the island."

"We thought it might be Thompson," Aaron explains, "but look." He points behind us, where we came from. "See that light? It's the caretaker doing his safety walk. He always has a flashlight." Sure enough, a light flickers in the distance. I turn back to the lighthouse and it's pitch black once again.

"We've tried everything," Tia says. "Now it's up to you. Find out who the shadow is, and you can join our club. You have three days."

Chapter 7

In all the mystery books I've read, the detective always lays out the facts: who, what, where, when, why. Although I'm a little scared to have the responsibility of this mystery no one can solve, I'm also a little excited.

Back in the hut, I ask for some paper and pen.

"We have a chalkboard," Gaby says, jumping to her feet.

"I'm the only one who uses that chalkboard," Tia says, folding her arms.

Gaby stops mid-walk. "So… don't get her the chalkboard… ?" she asks.

Tia sits behind her desk and shoots a glare at Gaby. "If she wants to use it, then I should be the one to give her permission, don't you think?"

Gaby takes two steps back to her beanbag and plumps down, her lips upturned. I frown at Tia; I don't know what her deal is and why she treats everyone this way. Does she own the island? Aren't they her friends?

Tia catches me looking at her, and nods over to the far wall. "You can use the chalkboard," she says.

My automatic reaction is to curtsy, treat her like the queen she thinks she is, but I think it might be too soon to disrupt the group and by the look of the twins' earnest faces, they're begging me not to embarrass them.

"So?" she says, as I move the chalkboard to the centre of the room. "How are you going to solve the mystery?"

I'm facing the board and use the opportunity to make a grimacing face that she can't see, before taking a breath and turning to face her and the others. "I need more than five minutes to solve this," I tell her, trying hard to control my temper. "All you did was show me a shadow."

"The shadow is the mystery, and your cousins said you could solve it," she snaps back. "So can you solve it or not?"

I fold my arms, squeezing the chalk tightly between my fingers. "Can you?" I raise my eyebrows at her.

"I think, maybe, Fayson might need more than an hour?" Gaby suggests. Tia refocuses her glare from me to Gaby.

"And you did give her three days," Aaron adds, flashing me what seems like a sympathetic smile.

Tia turns back to me. "So, you have nothing? No hunches or suggestions?"

This feels like a setup. Like she wants me to fail.

I point to the chalkboard as if to remind her how this all started. "You haven't given me much to go on but a shadow and a light... but it's a start." I turn my back to them and write in block letters across the board:

THE MYSTERIOUS SHADOW IN THE LIGHTHOUSE

"So, tell me everything you know so far— when did it start, where did it start, and what happened..." I turn to them, like a teacher teaching a class on how to be a detective.

"It started in the last school holidays," Aaron says.

"About three months ago," Ace adds.

"Tia noticed from her house, because they have three floors and she has a balcony in her bedroom," Gaby adds.

"I can see everything from that balcony," Tia says smugly.

"She called us, and we all raced to see what it was," Omar joins in. "It was a really boring holiday break, I remember."

"But then it disappeared when we got there," Tia says. "So I got the group to take turns looking out for it. Omar and Aaron went first. They were the first ones to notice that it happened at the same time. Then Gaby and Ace did the same thing and I realized that it was happening every night."

"I noticed," Omar moaned. "It was me and Aaron."

Tia ignores him. "I put all the clues together, then I arranged for us to wait one night to try and catch who it was." She rolls her eyes, nodding towards the group. "But they fell asleep."

Gaby raises her hand, but Tia pays her no mind.

"We even went into the lighthouse in the

day to look around, but we couldn't find anything."

Gaby leans towards me. "I didn't fall asleep," she whispers. "Tia sent me on a food errand."

Tia shoots her a glare, acknowledging her for the first time. "Gaby, it's very rude to talk when I'm talking."

Gaby mumbles an apology under her breath.

"So the light flashes every night?" I ask, adding thoughts to the board. I wish I had a hat. Detectives always wear hats.

Tia nods. "Every day, the same time. Nothing changes. We can predict it down to the second. You just need to do what we couldn't—find out who or what is doing it, and why."

I feel a surge of excitement and importance as they throw answers at me. This is it. This is my dream. I am a real-life detective! Not a pretend one like I am back home. This is real.

I am important. This is what I have been waiting for my whole life.

Even with Tia's eyes piercing into me… even she cannot stop the way I feel right now. I am going to solve this, just you watch me, Tia!

Uncle Edmond doesn't come to dinner that evening, even though a place is set out for him on the long wooden table facing the pool. Elma bustles round the table placing bowls of food in front of us.

"Where's Daddy?" Omar asks, the last to sit down. He's changed his clothes to another polo shirt, just blue this time instead of white. His mother sits at the head of the table, but she may as well be sitting in another room for how far away she is. She's also dressed up, and as I look around me, I notice they have all changed into dressier clothes, as though they were going to see the Prime Minister or something. I look down at myself, still wearing the same clothes I arrived in, and wrap my arms round myself.

"He's working," Aunty Desiree says, placing a napkin on her lap. I copy her, doing the same.

"You always say that," Omar hisses under his breath.

"So, any thoughts on the case yet?" Aaron whispers. For some reason he has decided to sit right beside me, ignoring the other six chairs at the table.

I do have thoughts. Lots of them. But none has brought me any closer to figuring out the puzzle of the shadow in the lighthouse.

Elma fills my plate with food without asking, when I really wanted to taste everything first because some of the food looks alien to me.

"Why did you tell them I could solve it?" I ask him, changing the subject. I poke a fork in some green thing that looks like a miniature tree.

"That's broccoli," Aunty Desiree says, nodding to me. "Flown in from England."

"You buy a tree from England to eat it?" I ask baffled. They all snort, just like they did on the phone when I didn't know where their island was.

"It's a vegetable," she answers through her laugh. "It's very good for you, try it." I pick the tiny tree up with my fork and sniff it, which sends the boys laughing again. This time I've had enough. I can feel my blood boiling.

"Why you always laughing like mi a comedian?" I snap. "I never tell you no joke and yuh laugh. I answer the phone, yuh laugh. I eat dis nasty tree, yuh laugh. And nothing is funny!"

I push my chair back and storm off out of the dining room and towards my room.

I hate when people laugh at me. It stirs something inside me. Something I can't control.

"It's rude to leave the table," Aunty Desiree calls after me.

I run into my room and shut the door behind me, being careful not to slam it. It's rude to laugh at people too, but they don't care about that.

I throw myself on to the high bed and stare at the ceiling. As my breath catches in my throat, I can hear Mama's voice in my ears—*Be good*—and now I feel sick knowing that I have already let her down.

A few minutes later, when I am sure I have managed to calm down, I return to the dinner table. It is quiet, apart from the sound of Omar's knife and fork scraping the plate. I pull the chair back and pause, looking over to Aunty Desiree, who is deep in her chicken and doesn't seem to notice me come back.

"I am sorry, Aunty," I say in my best English, because I know that's what they like. She looks up from her plate and her eyes are soft, but her eyebrows are raised as if waiting for something else. Her red lipstick has stained her fork and looks like she's bleeding, but I don't say that because I don't think that's what she wants to hear right now.

"I am very sorry for my rudeness and for leaving the table, and for shouting."

She nods with a smile, and I take that as 'sit down', so I do.

"Also, we don't smell our food," she says, still smiling. "But we will teach you everything you need to know, won't we, boys?" She says the last bit sternly, glaring at Omar, who has a piece of chicken in his hand, his mouth all greasy.

Omar slowly lowers the chicken to his plate and mumbles, 'Yes, Mummy.'

When we have finished eating, I go to get up from the table, but Aaron stops me. He nods to his mother, who wipes her mouth with a napkin, places it on the table beside her, then pushes her chair back. She stands, then turns and leaves. As she turns the corner, Aaron's hand drops off my leg.

I glare at him. "You know, if a boy did that back home, I would bite his hand off."

His eyes widen as he places his napkin on the table just the way his mum did. "Bit dramatic," he mumbles, getting up from the table. "Just trying to help."

Omar looks over at me from the other side of the table. "So, have you come up with anything yet? We don't have much time."

I frown, realizing they're not going to give me a minute's peace with this case. "I need to go the tower," I say, trying to sound important.

"The lighthouse," Omar corrects me.

I ignore him, looking only at his brother. "You think your mother will let us go there, to have a look?"

Aaron smiles, bemused. "Yes, of course," he says. "Let's go ask her."

We make the same journey towards the lighthouse, only this time we don't cut off into the bushes, we follow the road round.

It's now late evening and the moon is bright in the sky. It shines down on us like a torch lighting the road ahead. The road is empty as usual. It's taking me some time to get used to it, but the twins walk confidently in the middle of the road. Omar is beatboxing to some song and walking a little ahead of us, with a dip in his step.

"He's okay, you know," Aaron says, catching me giving his brother an evil look.

"Once you get to know him again, you'll see. He's just weird with new people, or people he hasn't seen in a while."

I raise one eyebrow. "He seems the same as when he threw a spider in my bed two years ago." I take a second to assess Aaron. "You seem a little different though. You seem… less annoying."

He does a double take. "Me?" he says, pointing at himself.

I tut, shaking my head. "No, the ghost standing behind you." He looks behind himself, pretending to be scared, then breaks into a laugh and I can't help but laugh with him.

The road comes to an end and beyond it are nothing but rocks. Further ahead, the lighthouse looms before us. In the distance, to our right, I notice the place where we hid before. Omar stops suddenly and I bump into him.

"Watch it!" he snaps.

I stare up at the towering building, which is like a twenty-foot white cone with glass windows at the top. There is no sound around us, no movement, no other person but us. I glance behind me nervously, then back at the building.

"So, what now?" Aaron says hesitantly. I can feel my heart pounding against my chest as I think of all the things that could go wrong here. We are too far from the house for anyone to hear us scream, and the lighthouse is eerie. The way it towers over us with the moon above it feels threatening, as though it's warning us to enter at our own risk.

"Well?" Omar asks quietly.

I clear my throat. "We should... probably... you know... maybe..."

They stare at me blankly.

"Go in?" Aaron's voice wavers. Even Omar doesn't seem so sure, but this is my case. This is what I wanted, isn't it? To be an FBI agent and solve mysteries. I've spent hours in my room preparing for this day, and now it is real. I can't fail now, not when everyone is relying on me.

Be brave, Fayson!

I take a deep breath, clasping my fingers together to hide the shaking. I nod. "Yes, we should go in."

I push past Omar and over to the brown door. I wrap my fingers round the black metal handle, take another deep breath and turn it.

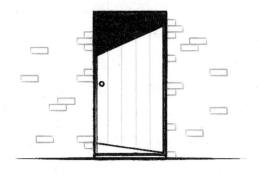

Chapter 8

The door creaks open like an old, abandoned house. I let go of the handle and the door swings back against the stone wall. Inside is a small oval entrance that curves up from the foot of a black iron staircase. The staircase twists like a snake, upwards into the roof of the lighthouse.

I hear my heart pounding hard against my chest as I sweep the room with my eyes, looking for anyone or anything that could be hiding.

Omar pushes me from behind. "Go on then. You're the detective, and detectives always go first."

"If she's the detective, what are we?" Aaron asks his brother from behind me. "Sidekicks?"

"You might be her sidekick, but I'm not," Omar scoffs.

I ignore them, stepping gingerly towards the bottom step. I look up, craning my neck to see, but the winding staircase hides what is at the top.

"I'll be Batman and you be Robin," Omar says.

"That..." Aaron sighs, "that won't work."

"Why not?" Omar snaps.

I spin round and I glare at him, placing my fingers on my lips.

"Why not?" he whispers to his brother.

"Because it's not a superhero movie," Aaron hisses. "And if it was, I would never be Robin. You would be Robin."

I look at the first step leading upwards, trying to bring myself to stand on it. The gaps in between each one don't seem safe, and it's hard to imagine what's at the top. Anyone or anything could be waiting, and the odds would be against us. They would already have the advantage of knowing we were coming.

The door bangs behind me, making me jump, and I spin round to see Omar and Aaron inside with the door closed behind them.

"Whoo-hoo," Omar cries, wriggling his fingers at me in what must be his attempt at a ghost. He laughs hysterically. "You look like you're going to pee your pants," he says, laughing even harder.

Suddenly a noise from above stops him mid laugh. We all freeze, staring at each other.

"What was that?" Aaron whispers. Our heads tilt slowly up towards the top of the lighthouse. There it is again—another noise, like a tin pot banging against the wall. I step on to the first stair cautiously, my hand hovering over the banister.

"I think we should go home now," Omar whispers.

With my heart in my mouth, I continue up, barely making a sound. I don't know what I'm going to find, or what I'll do when I get there.

I don't check if the boys are following. It's like something has come over me. I need to solve this mystery, and this sound might give us the answer we have been looking for.

I'm not going to be afraid, I tell myself, on every step that takes me closer to the top. *I'm not going to be afraid. I am going to be brave. I am Fayson FBI.*

The further up the stairs I go, the further away I am from the front door, and escape. I try to remember what my favourite detective would do if someone was at the top of the stairs waiting. But my favourite detective was so good at her job that no one ever knew when she was coming. She was silent as the night.

The last turn of the staircase approaches. I glance upwards to the roof of the lighthouse, looking for a light or a shadow, but nothing.

A sudden bang behind me stops me in my tracks.

I turn to see Omar's phone flying down the stairs, through the gap and hitting the ground.

His hands fly to his head. He looks up at both me and Aaron, his eyes wide. His mouth hangs open. We all turn to look towards the top of the stairs... and wait.

I hold my hand out to stop them from making another move. We listen. For feet. A voice. Anything. But there is nothing.

I quicken my steps to the top. When I reach the last step, my heart is in my mouth expecting to see something waiting for us.

But the small landing is empty. I turn to Aaron and Omar, who are both close behind. There is a door in front of us, which I'm sure leads to the room where we saw the shadow earlier. I rock on my feet, willing myself to open it.

Come on, Fayson. You can do this. It's only a door. No one is behind it.

I count to three in my head, take a quick breath and fling the door open.

It swings back, hitting the wall behind.

The room is empty. Ahead of us is the window, circling the entire room. Slightly to the left is a dusty bookcase that hasn't seen a cleaning rag in probably a hundred years. Or a book for that matter. I step inside and look around. I can see the sea. At night it looks grey instead of blue.

I scan the room. Nothing. I notice one of the side windows is open, and the breeze from the sea blows in, slamming the door behind us. I sigh in relief as I realize what the banging was.

"It's the wind," I tell them, walking over to the window and closing it. From this height I can see more of the main island, and it's filled with tiny lights that look like peenie wallies, those bugs with insides that light up.

I think of Mama and what she must be doing now. Then I remember how she said she would call me. I feel in my pocket for my phone, but it's not there. I left it back at the house! I start to panic that I may have missed her call, so I turn and begin running back down, passing the boys on the stairs.

"Where are you going?" Aaron shouts, baffled.

"I don't want to miss Mama's call," I cry. I hear their thundering feet behind me.

"But what about the shadow?" Omar shouts back. I reach the ground floor and fling the door open, grateful to see the outside again.

Omar runs to get his phone and cries out when he sees it on the floor. "Oh no," he says, staring at it in dismay. The phone has a large crack along its case.

On our way back, he moans the entire way.

"I can't get another phone now until I'm sixteen. Daddy said if I break it, I don't get another one." He groans out loud. "I didn't even want to come on this stupid trip, and it was a waste of time. We didn't even

do anything, and I still broke my phone."
He shoots me a look. "You're the worst
detective."

"Then you shouldn't have called me to
come here," I snap back, quickening my pace
to get away from him.

"I won't be calling you again," he shouts
after me. "You suck!"

I bite my lip, holding my head straight,
my arms swinging wildly as I widen the gap
between us. The truth is, he is right. I have
failed. I thought I was being brave going into
the lighthouse. I was so sure that being here
would help me solve the mystery.

For once, Omar and I agree on something:
I don't think I'm meant to be a detective
after all.

Tia calls a meeting the next day. She sends
everyone a secret message, apparently, but

I don't get it because I'm not in the group yet. Aaron and Omar find me reading just outside my room. I'm on the veranda that wraps round the entire back of the house.

"What are you reading?" Aaron asks, slumping into a wicker chair next to me. I show him the cover of my mystery book. It's one I've read a hundred times. He squints at the cover.

"*Hazley and Barnaby Save The World*," he reads. "Is it good?"

"Who cares!" Omar interrupts, throwing his hands up in the air. "Let's go. Tia's called a meeting."

I place a bookmark in the page I'm reading. "Why?"

Omar groans. "Because she's the leader and she can." He starts walking down the garden. Aaron follows and I'm a step behind him.

"So, no sweaty blindfold this time?" I joke.

"I wasn't sweaty," Omar mutters from the front. "Besides, that was only if Tia didn't want you to solve the case, but she does, so…" He shrugs and his voice trails off.

When we enter the hut, the others are already there. *Did Tia collect everyone on her way here, or did they wait for her at her front door like obedient members*, I wonder.

"So? What do you have for us?" Tia asks, sitting behind her desk, her arms folded and her head tilted to one side. The others follow her lead and look at me for answers.

"I need more time," I tell her.

She sighs, shaking her head. "How much more time?"

I glare at her. "Well, you did give me three days… I don't know… Three days?"
I flash her a smile.

She isn't impressed and turns to the twins, her eyebrows raised.

"We did go to the lighthouse last night, didn't we?" Aaron says, nodding at me.

"Yeah, we heard a noise," Omar adds.

Tia sits forward. "A noise?"

Omar nods his head. "But then I dropped my phone, and it doesn't work so I don't have a phone any more." He takes it out of his pocket and shows the room, like a show and tell.

"Oh no," Gaby cries, leaning over him to take a closer look. "Won't your father buy you a new one?"

Omar shakes his head but is jolted back with Tia's loud sigh.

"No one cares about your old phone," she snaps. "Tell me about the noise."

Omar mumbles under his breath that's it's not old, but Tia ignores him, turning to me. "What noise?"

I shrug. "A banging noise, I don't know, it came from the top but there was nothing there."

"Maybe a ghost?" Ace suggests, speaking for the first time today. He shrugs when everyone looks at him. "It was always what we thought, so it makes sense."

I shake my head. "It was the wind, I think. The window was open."

Tia's eyebrows crease as she stares at me. Then she turns to Aaron. "Do you think it was a ghost?"

Aaron shrugs. "It could be the wind, but it sounded different."

Tia nods. "I think it was a ghost too."

I sigh, annoyed at not being listened to. "Or it was the wind?" I repeat.

For a moment she says nothing. Just looks at me and I can't read her expression.

"Well, you know best," she says to my surprise. "You are the most experienced of all of us. So, what do you think? What if it isn't a ghost?" she says. "How do you explain the shadow?"

I'm surprised that she cares for my opinion and it's the first time Tia seems genuinely interested in anything I have to say.

"Well," I say slowly, thinking I may be able to redeem my detective status. "There's only one way to find out."

She raises her eyebrows at me.

"We need to spend the night there," I say, my heart beating fast as the idea forms in my head. "It's the only way to know for sure. We get there before the shadow, and catch them in the act."

Silence falls around me and Tia's eyebrows crease together, her lips moving from side to side.

"All night?" Gaby says hesitantly.

I nod, becoming surer the more I think about it. It's what my favourite detective would do. She would stake out the place until she caught the culprit red-handed.

"I like it," Aaron says, nodding approval.

Ace agrees, nodding his head too. "Sounds like a plan."

"I don't know…" Gaby says, biting her nails.

"Can everyone be quiet!" Tia shouts, holding her hand out. Everyone stops talking, just like they did yesterday. Doing exactly as they're told.

She sits back in her chair, stroking her chin like an old man trying to figure out what he wants for dinner. I wait, my heart beating fast. She sits forward and nods her head slowly.

"I agree," she says at last. "We should spend the night in the lighthouse."

Chapter 9

"You ask him! He won't say no to you."
Aaron pushes me forwards to the door of
Uncle Edmond's office, where he seems to
spend all his time even though the whole
family is meant to be on holiday.

We had already asked Aunty Desiree a few
minutes ago, but unlike yesterday when she
allowed us to go to the lighthouse, this time
she wasn't so sure.

"You know I'm all for you having your
little adventures and getting out from under

my feet," she said as she dug up dirt in their garden. She was wearing a wide-brimmed hat that covered her face and matched her green vest and green shorts. I had stared at her, wondering if rich people ever dress like normal people. Then she waved a gloved hand towards the house. "Overnight is a different thing altogether. It's not me you have to convince for this one."

So the boys had dragged their feet to the house, playing a pointing game to work out who would be the one to talk to him.

Now we are standing outside Uncle Edmond's office, too afraid to go in. I know why I'm afraid—I don't think Uncle Edmond likes me very much—but I'm surprised at the twins, who seem to get whatever they want, whenever they ask for it. My hand is raised, but I haven't knocked yet.

"Why would he say yes to me?" I ask, confused. Omar and Aaron exchange glances. I glare at them both, repeating the question.

"We heard him say that he wants you to have such a good time that it will make his sister jealous and want to come here too," Omar tells me.

I stare at him blankly. "What?"

They glance at each other again. "I think it's his way of trying to get closer to your mum."

"But... they're not close because you are always travelling."

Aaron shakes his head. "It's because your mum doesn't answer his calls."

"But she answered the call about me coming here," I say indignantly.

Aaron nods. "Yes. It was our call, from our phone."

I roll my eyes, turning my back on them and facing the door. This is just another of their tricks, making things up so I'll do their dirty work. I know Mama and Uncle Edmond don't talk as much as they used to, but the twins stopped talking to me too. They didn't speak to me for a year, then dragged me to this island to solve a case they couldn't solve themselves. I'm tired of doing their dirty work!

I lower my hand and step back, folding my arms. "He's your father. You ask him."

Omar sighs. "You'll see," he warns me. "Then you'll be sorry you messed it up for all of us."

I fume behind him, as he knocks on the wooden door.

"Is that you, Elma? I hope you have my tea," Uncle Edmond calls from behind the door.

Omar shoots us a look. "We should have brought his tea!" Aaron hisses.

"He'll be much nicer with his tea," Omar agrees, and so we rush down the hall towards the kitchen. As we turn the corner, we bump into a startled Elma, nearly toppling the tea tray she is carrying.

"We'll take that, Elma," Aaron says, prying the tray out of her hand. Before she has time to answer, we turn on our heels and head back to the office.

Omar knocks again, breathing heavily from running.

"Come in." Uncle Edmond sounds a little annoyed this time, which only makes us more nervous. We glance at each other, feeling a little uncertain.

Omar opens the door and lets his brother enter first with the tea. It works. Uncle Edmond's eyes light up.

"What is this? Do I have new staff?" he jokes, as Aaron places the tray on his desk. We wait while he pours himself a cup and takes a biscuit, placing it in the saucer.

"Right, what do you want?" he says, looking up. "Whatever it is, I can't afford it."

Aaron clasps his hands in front of him, getting ready to speak, but Omar gets there before him.

"Daddy, we want to spend a night in the lighthouse."

My uncle frowns, stirring his tea. "The lighthouse? Why?"

"Because Fayson wants to," Omar blurts out. I shoot him a deathly stare. "She's never been in a lighthouse before, and she wants to see what it is like."

He glances over to me. "That true, Fayson?"

I feel Omar's elbow in my side and I clench my teeth. Then I take a breath, to remind myself to reply in 'proper' English. "Yes, Uncle, it's true."

He stops stirring and looks at me. "We have talked about your pronunciation before, haven't we?"

My head falls to my chest. A long, low sigh escapes me. "Yes, Uncle, it's true," I repeat in my best English voice.

He raises one eyebrow. "We'll work on that."

I can feel my cheeks burning and I avoid looking at the twins, who are probably enjoying every minute of this.

Uncle Edmond takes a slow sip of his tea and all we can hear in the room is his slurping. He places the cup down. "You boys look after her. I don't want my sister getting mad at me because she got lost up there." He chuckles, reaching for the phone. "I'll tell Thompson to check in on you during his rounds."

I am barely listening to what he is saying. Instead, I am still thinking about why Uncle Edmond always wants to upset me.

"Yes, Daddy," both boys say at once. They leave the room in a flash. I pause just behind them, lingering on Uncle Edmond's face, which is now deep in concentration. He doesn't look like Mama. Her skin is soft; his is hard and wrinkled. His face is square like a box, and Mama's is rounded like a mango.

If anyone's not talking, it's him not talking to Mama. He seems the type to do that. He seems the type to give up on family.

He catches me looking at him. "Anything else, Fayson?"

I blush, shaking my head. "No, Uncle." I leave hurriedly.

Later that morning, Elma takes us to the back of the house, at the end of the hall by Omar's room, where there is a tall floor-to-ceiling cupboard that blends into the white walls. Elma takes out a bunch of keys from her pocket and unlocks the cupboard.

"I have to keep it locked or these boys will take everything in here," she explains to me.

I peer inside. It is a large walk-in wardrobe, almost as big as my room back home! The wardrobe has rows of shelves along each side wall, all filled with boxes. Along the floor are old shoes, a couple of surfboards and water flippers. On the far wall, coats and goggles hang, along with wetsuits.

Someone switches on a light and the room brightens. Elma walks to a far side of the room and pulls two boxes down to the ground. "These have your sleeping bags and old blankets in," she says, flicking one open. "There should be some flashlights in there too."

We rush over to the boxes and begin pulling things out excitedly, then we spend the rest of the day getting ready for our night adventure.

On the way to the lighthouse, I can't stop thinking about what the twins said about Mama and Uncle Edmond. I always thought we didn't see them any more because they were always travelling, but now I'm beginning to wonder if it was something else.

It is strange that they only lived on the other side of the island and yet didn't drive to see us but did get on planes to other countries. Sometimes I was relieved I didn't have to deal with their tricks, and at other times I felt hurt by it. I never told anyone that.

I walk a little behind the brothers, watching as they talk among themselves. They're each wearing a backpack over their shoulders, filled with snacks and blankets in case it gets cold.

As we enter the path to the lighthouse, I can see the others already waiting by the lighthouse door. Tia looks at us with disapproval when we approach.

"Five o'clock, we said." She checks her phone, and Aaron and Omar lower their heads like naughty children.

"We had to ask our dad," Aaron mumbles.

"Well, first we asked our mum," Omar interrupts, "but she told us to ask our dad… But then we got him some tea to get him on our side, and then we told Fayson to do it, because he would never say no to her, and—"

Tia shoves her hand in his face. "Stop talking," she whispers, seething. "You're making my head hurt."

Omar stares at his feet and I want to tell him not to do that, even though I don't like Omar and we don't get along. He is my cousin, and I hate seeing him bullied like this.

She turns her attention to me. "You're supposed to be leading. This is your initiation into the group. You should be here before all of us. Or are you giving up already?"

I sigh. "You would like that, wouldn't you?" I push past Tia, and in front of the rest of them. "Everybody ready?" I ask, before turning the handle and flinging the door open.

Chapter 10

Inside, the lighthouse seems less scary now it's light and there are more of us. Or maybe it's because I am too busy thinking about Tia's face when I barged past her.

We stand at the bottom of the stairs looking around us, for what, I don't know. Gaby links arms with me.

"You're doing so well," she whispers, giving my arm a squeeze. "Don't listen to anyone that tells you any different." By 'anyone', I take it she means Tia, who is now over by Ace, asking him why he didn't bring a blanket.

"Why does she talk like an adult?" I ask Gaby.

She rolls her eyes. "Because she's older than the rest of us by six months."

I start to climb the stairs, with Gaby still holding on to me, and the others follow. "And why does she have so much power over everyone?" I ask quietly. She seems to be the only one willing to talk about this.

"Her father owns Lighthouse Island," Gaby whispers under her breath. "Only Mrs Hammond, who lives on the other side, and Thompson live here permanently. Everyone else is only here for the holidays. Every time we do something Tia doesn't like, she threatens to tell her father to kick us off."

I slow down as we reach the top, desperate to know more. "So, they can kick you off anytime they want?" I say in disbelief.

Gaby shrugs. "I think so... None of us want to find out, anyway. That's why we don't upset her. She's threatened to tell her father before, so we let her say and do what she wants."

We reach the top of the winding stairs, and I look behind me to see where Tia is. As I look down, her eyes look directly back at me and she's not smiling. Maybe that's why she dislikes me so much: she has no control over me. I'm just here for this holiday.

At the top of the lighthouse, I lead the group into the room with the big, sweeping window at the front, stretching out my arms either side of me to stop them going any further.

"We should stay away from the window," I warn them. "There may be clues." Instead I lead them behind the old bookcase. In the dark, it will hide us but still give us a chance to spot whoever enters the room.

I settle into the corner nearest to the door. There's a small gap between the bookcase and the wall, where I can peek out to see who comes in and who leaves. As I slide on to the floor, Tia crawls over to me.

"That space should be mine," she says. She sighs when I just stare at her blankly. "The leader gets first choice, and I choose this spot."

I look around me, baffled, then back at her. "Which part is your name at?" I ask her, falling back into Patwah. I point to the wall. "Show me where it says 'Tia's spot' on these walls."

Her face contorts and she looks around her to see everyone is listening. She leans into me. "Do you know who I am? My father owns this entire island. So yes, my name is on all these walls—so *move it*."

Tia shoves me out of the way, forcing herself into the space. I catch Aaron shaking his head at me as I open my mouth to tell her what I think of her and her island. I bite my lip hard, grab my things and crawl over to the other side, between Aaron and Gaby.

Gaby lays a gentle hand on me. "Don't worry," she whispers. "She can't be leader for ever, right?"

I glare over at Tia, who's busy setting herself up in my area. "Well, her father owns the island," I say, mimicking her voice, "so she's going to be leader for ever, until you all die of old age. Not me though," I say bitterly. "I get to leave and go home, and will probably never come back here."

"Well, maybe these few weeks can change our whole lives," she says, beaming.

I don't know what she means by that. I don't know how me, a poor girl from the city, can make any difference to these rich people and their lives. But I'm beginning to think being rich isn't everything. In fact, I think being at home with my fake detective stories is much better than getting bossed around by Tia.

We have been waiting for an hour, eating snacks and constantly checking the time, when Tia claps her hands to get everyone's attention. Everyone stares at her and for once she is smiling, but her smile makes me feel uncomfortable. More uncomfortable than this cold, hard floor we're sitting on.

"Fayson, you never told us where you're from," she says, the creepy smile fixed on her face. I shift uncomfortably, feeling everyone's eyes on me. Aaron and Omar's gazes are particularly piercing.

"I'm from the city," I tell her, matter of fact.

She laughs. "No, silly, we're from the city. Where are *you* from?"

I bite my lip, remembering what Mama said: to be good. I know what Tia's doing. She wants me to admit that I'm poor and don't belong here. She wants to embarrass me.

"Montego Bay," I answer coldly.

She leans forward, her arms wrapped round her knees. "Where in Montego Bay? We have a house there. Rose Hall? The Lagoons?" She continues to reel off neighbourhoods—all rich, all with big mansions and swimming pools. All places I have only seen from afar. All places Mama and I could never afford.

"You wouldn't know it," Aaron says, interrupting her.

Tia glares at him. "I know everywhere," she snaps. Her eyes return to me, and that fake smile returns with it. "So? Where is it? Where do you live?"

"I live in the city," I tell her sharply. "By the library, next to the shopping centre."

The twins hang their heads, as though I've revealed their darkest secret. And that's when I realize: they are ashamed of me.

They don't want their rich friends to know I live in an apartment block beside a busy road next to a shopping centre. They especially don't want Tia to know Mama is a nurse who works all night and yet we still can't afford anything better.

Tia stares at me in disbelief. A short laugh escapes her. "No one lives by a shopping centre," she says. Then her eyes widen, and her mouth falls open. "Are you... poor?"

Something about the way she says it hits me in the heart. In that moment, I feel worthless. I have never wanted anything but Mama's time. I love our apartment; it's cosy and I have my own room, which I didn't have before when we lived in the country. Back then, in our old family house, Mama and I shared a room, so when we moved in the apartment was a luxury by comparison. I could see the ocean from my bedroom window, behind the palm tree, behind the road, over the wall. It was closer than we had ever been to the coast, and we didn't need to take a bus to get there. Mama had said how lucky we were to have the sea so close. I felt lucky, but not here. Here I feel like dirt.

The sound of an alarm interrupts the awkward silence. I scramble to turn it off, in case it spooks the shadow. We freeze for a second, waiting for what, I don't know. Running of feet as the shadow escapes into the night? But there is nothing but silence.

"It's time," I tell them quietly, unable to look anyone in the eye. "Two minutes until the shadow appears. We should wait for it to go to the window. Ace, you lock the door so he can't escape. Then we find out who it is."

Everyone except Tia nods. Then we settle

down to wait but I can still feel Tia's eyes on me. I can imagine her smug grin.

Time passes slowly. The silence is heavy. I beg the shadow to make an appearance, just to take the attention off me. So that we can go back to the real reason we are here: to solve the mystery.

Two minutes pass. Then five. Then ten. Then twenty. Nothing happens. No shadow. No flashing lights. There is only the sound of the wind outside, swirling round the lighthouse.

The room becomes darker and colder as the moon hides behind a cloud. I pull the blanket Elma gave me over my shoulders and under my legs. One by one, people settle into their blankets or coats, or whatever they have brought with them, and then, tired of waiting, people start falling asleep. Aaron curls up on the floor by my feet and Gaby's sleeping head falls on to my shoulder.

I check my phone. Eleven o'clock. We have been here for over five hours.

I look around me. Everyone is asleep except Tia. She leans against the wall getting comfortable. I lean my head against the wall too, determined not to fall asleep. Now more than ever I need to solve this case, if only just to shove it in Tia's smug face.

But my eyes grow heavy and eventually I can't keep them open any longer.

I don't know how long I slept for, but a strange sound wakes me. I open my eyes, disorientated at first, then remember where I am and feel mad at myself for falling asleep.

I look around. Everyone is still sleeping. Everyone except Tia, who is typing on her phone. I hear the sound again and sit upright. Tia and I exchange looks. It's footsteps, coming up the stairs.

I nudge Gaby beside me.

"Egg and toast please, Mummy," she mumbles. I nudge again, and she jolts awake. Aaron sits up slowly, as though the noise woke him too, but Omar and Ace are still fast asleep.

The footsteps reach the top of the stairs and stop outside the closed door. Gaby grips me as the door handle turns slowly. I glance down at my phone.

1.05 a.m. Six and a half hours after the shadow's usual time.

My heart is in my mouth as the door creaks open slowly, waking Omar and Ace. I wait with bated breath as the door swings back. It's hard to tell if there's anyone standing there. It could be a dark figure, or it could just be my imagination. I rub my eyes and look again.

No, it definitely is a dark figure. Tall, adult tall, dressed from head to toe in black.

Tia jumps out of her hiding place screaming, "Got you!" at the top of her voice. The figure immediately disappears back down the stairs. I jump to my feet to chase after him, the others following closely behind. I skip down the steps, barely touching each one, just as the figure vanishes round the winding staircase.

I can hear Tia shouting, "Get him, Fayson!" The others join her, cheering me on. I race down to the bottom of the stairs and to the ground floor.

It's empty.

I spin round, confused. Where did he go? The front door was closed, and I didn't hear it open just now. By the time the others have joined me, I am checking every corner of the room for a secret door.

"Where did he go?" Aaron cries.

"Fayson let him go," Tia huffs.

I turn to her angrily. "Why did you do that?" I cry, frustrated.

She looks at me blankly. "Do what?"

"Shout out! We were supposed to wait for him to come into the room, and lock him in so he couldn't escape."

She laughs a short laugh. "So then we're stuck in a room with the shadow? That's smart."

"Tia's right," Gaby agrees, clasping her hands together nervously. "It could be dangerous, Fayson, you don't know what it would have done." The others nod in agreement.

I take a breath, biting my bottom lip. "If you didn't like the idea, why didn't you say so when I suggested it?"

She sighs, rolling her eyes. "We don't have time for this, Fayson. I'm going to get Thompson to search the area. The shadow can't have gone far."

"Or he might have left some evidence," Gaby suggests eagerly.

I move around the room, staring at the ground. "Look!" I point down by the entrance. "Footprints."

Everyone directs the light of their phones to the floor and sure enough there are lots of footprints, all going in different directions. Excited chatter fills the room.

"You can identify people from footprints," I tell them, remembering the clues from another of my favourite books, *The Mysterious Case of The Jewellery Thief*. "Thompson can take a picture and check everyone's shoes."

To my surprise, Tia agrees. "I'll go and get him," she says, opening the door.

"It's after one in the morning," I remind her. "Won't he be asleep?"

She looks at me weirdly. "No, he's the caretaker." She leaves before I can answer, closing the door behind her with a bang. But what I wanted to tell her was that caretakers sleep too!

"Does this mean the shadow is not a ghost?" Gaby says, breaking the silence.

"That was no ghost," I tell her with certainty. "That was a real person."

Chapter 11

What I'm learning about solving real mysteries is that you can spend hours, or days, trying to find a clue. Just one clue. Then as soon as you do, everything starts falling into place. Like a jigsaw, the more pieces you put together, the more you start to see the big picture.

Tia didn't take long to find Thompson. She came back with him within minutes, so he must have been close by.

"Our parents know we're here, before

you ask," Omar says, as soon as he enters. Thompson makes a 'humph' sound.

"You don't have anything better to do than keep bothering me with this?" he asks in a strong Patwah, which takes me aback for a second.

He looks at each of us, his eyes falling on me a little longer than everyone else. I am surprised Tia found him so quickly, and that he's here in the middle of the night, but soon I'm distracted by telling Thompson everything that has happened.

I tell him about the noise, then the shadow. I tell him how I chased the shadow to here, to the door of the lighthouse, but it was gone. And how I am certain they didn't leave via the lighthouse door.

Surprisingly, Tia doesn't interrupt, which isn't like her at all. As I get to the part about the footprints, the caretaker shines his torch on to the ground.

"These footprints?" he says, flashing light at the shoe marks going in different directions.

I nod, feeling important and like I might have broken a long-standing case.

He circles the room, his torch following the footsteps, and I wait for him to take out his phone and take a picture to start the investigation. He stops and looks at me tiredly. "And who are you?"

"I told you," Tia says from across the room, "she's Omar and Aaron's poor cousin."

I feel my body tense and I avoid her eyes, but I know she's waiting for a reaction.

Thompson sighs. "Well, Omar and Aaron's cousin…"

"Poor cousin," Tia adds.

Thompson ignores her. "These footprints," he says, "are yours."

I frown, staring at the ground in disbelief. I shake my head. "No." I look more carefully, tracking them across the floor. "Okay, maybe some are, but not all of them. And the case—"

He sighs again, walking over to the door, the dust footprints of his own boots covering all the others. "Your 'case' isn't a case, so maybe you can go home and get some sleep."

Thompson leaves, closing the door behind him. As I scan the room with my torch on, his footprints catch my eye and I frown. Something doesn't make sense. By torchlight, I follow the footprints that trail up the stairs, carefully studying each step, trying to distinguish which ones are ours and which could be the shadow's.

I follow the mixture of footprints all the way to the top of the stairs and into the room where we were hiding. Then I walk into the middle of the room and flash my phone torch to the floor there.

Slowly, I move towards the window and stop. I look out the window to the right, where we watched the shadow two days ago. Where he would have stood when we were watching from outside. I look down at the floor, and there are only one set of footprints here.

I take a photo with my phone; my mind is reeling. A hundred thoughts swim in my brain, none of them making sense. I am still thinking about it as I head back down to where the others are waiting.

Tia turns to me smugly. "Well, that was a waste of time," she says, heading for the door. "It's your deadline soon, Fayson. Are you giving up now, or are you going to drag it out until the end?"

I shake my head. "I'm not giving up," I say, my brain ticking as thoughts piece together. "I'll tell you who the shadow is tomorrow, when my time is up."

She looks at me strangely, then opens the door and leaves.

Gaby comes over to me, her eyes wide. "Tell me, who is it?"

I take out my phone and snap a few photos of the footprints around us. "Why don't you come over later today," I tell her. "I need your help."

I don't realize how I tired I am until my head hits the pillow. I sleep through breakfast, and wearily make it to lunch but only because Aunty Desiree sends Elma to wake me up.

At the table, Uncle Edmond is missing again, and the twins barely raise their heads to look at me. Aunty Desiree seems to enjoy laughing at our bleary eyes and tells Aaron to leave the blinds open when he tries to close them because it's too bright.

"I have no problem with you having your adventures," she says, "but you're not going to sleep the day away."

She bans us from going back to our rooms, so we drag our feet outside into the blaring sun and slump into the veranda furniture. Omar puts two chairs together and lies down. Aaron lays his legs over the arm of his chair and closes his eyes. I spread out on the only double seat and cover my eyes with my hoodie to block out the sun.

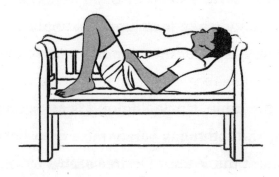

"Ms Gaby and Mr Ace are here," Elma announces. I squint out of my hood to see

Gaby and Ace looking just as tired as the rest of us. They drag two chairs from the other side of the veranda and sit down in silence.

"Your parents won't let you sleep either?" Aaron asks, opening one eye.

Ace sinks into the seat, resting his head on the back of the chair. "Parents are evil," he mutters.

Gaby tucks her feet under her and pulls her sunglasses over her eyes. "Is this what it feels like to be detectives?" she moans.

"Where's Tia?" I ask.

"Sleeping," they both respond together.

I sit up. "Don't you think it's weird how she tried to sabotage the plan last night?" I ask the group. They all look at each other, sharing something unsaid.

"I don't think she tried to sabotage it," Aaron says, squinting at me.

I sit forward on my chair. "But she warned the shadow. Why did she do that?"

Gaby shifts uncomfortably. "I don't think she did it on purpose."

I glare at her, wondering why she's suddenly changed her tune when she was on my side last night.

"We all shouted," Ace adds. "It wasn't just her."

I slump back in the chair, folding my arms firmly against my chest. Tia seems to have a hold on them even when she isn't around.

"I think she's trying to sabotage me," I mumble. "I don't think she wants me to solve this case."

"That doesn't make any sense," Omar grunts, leaning back against the chair and closing his eyes.

"You don't make any sense," I snap back, but he doesn't respond.

I look round at the others. Gaby is scrolling through her phone, Ace is taking his phone out of his pocket, but Aaron is staring at me, looking unconvinced.

"I'm not wrong," I tell him adamantly, because he's the only one listening, "You'll see." I lean back in the chair, frustrated.

Aunty Desiree comes into my room that evening to tell me there is a party at the Brookes' tonight and I must look my best.

When I ask her who the Brookes are she looks at me like I have three heads.

"The Brookes," she repeats, as if that helps.

"Tia," Aaron says, popping his head round the door. "Her family are the Brookes."

Now it all makes sense.

Aunty Desiree shows me three dresses. She says she bought them for me when she heard I was coming for the holidays, and I can't help but wonder why she thought she had to buy me clothes. Then I remember Tia calling me poor and realize they must all think that, even Aunty Desiree. They must think Mama can't even afford to buy me clothes.

"They aren't just the Brookes," she says, laying out a white dress, a light-blue dress and a dark-blue polka-dot one. "They are dear friends of ours, and this is a wonderful tradition we have. Everyone gets very excited for it." I catch Aaron rolling his eyes behind her.

Aunty Desiree picks up the white dress and holds it against me, tilting her head to the side. "It's the party of the holidays," she says, next holding up the light-blue dress, then the polka dot.

She nods. "Definitely the light blue." She glances over at the open door, where Aaron is watching, bemused. "Aaron, shouldn't you be getting ready?"

Aaron looks down at himself. "I am ready," he says, offended.

Aunty Desiree shakes her head, ushering him away. "No, the blue waistcoat and matching trousers please. The one I laid out for you."

"Please don't make me wear it! No one under twenty wears waistcoats," he moans, walking away.

Aunty Desiree shakes her head at me. "Boys, eh? Never do as they're told." I remain quiet as she asks me to try on a pair of black shoes, which I do obediently because I don't want her to tell Mama I was misbehaving, though they hurt my toes. "Yes, those for sure," she says.

She opens a box filled with jewellery, running her fingers through the pieces before picking a simple silver necklace.

"I've never worn a necklace," I tell her, as she places it round my neck. She smiles and I can feel her breath she's so close.

"Aren't you a lucky girl," she says, breathing on my skin as she speaks. Her breath is warm. "A private island for the holidays, the best party in the country, and you get all these beautiful things to wear."

She steps back to look at the necklace sitting on my chest.

"Beautiful," she purrs, "just beautiful." She grabs her things and heads for the door. "Be ready in twenty minutes," she says as she leaves. "We must be just late enough to make an entrance but not too late that anyone notices." She winks.

The door closes and I stay in the middle of the room, where she left me. The phone rings, jolting me out of my inertia, and I rush to pick it up. It's Mama.

"Mama!" I call down the phone.

"What are you doing?" she asks, and she sounds as though she is walking somewhere.

"Where are you going?" I ask, checking my phone for the time.

She laughs. "How you going to answer a question with a question, Fayson?" So I lie on the bed and tell her about the case of the shadow, and how it's going.

"So, you going to solve it in time?" she asks.

I roll on to my belly. "Mama, of course I'm going to solve it in time. In fact, I think I already have."

"Good," she says. "I'm happy to hear you're fitting in. I was worried you wouldn't."

I fall silent, wondering if I should tell her that I haven't really fitted in. That they see me as poor. That Tia hates me, and how when Tia hates someone, she makes your life hell. I want to tell her that Aunty Desiree treats me like charity. That Uncle Edmond doesn't think I can talk properly. But also, I don't want Mama to worry about me.

"So, what you are doing tonight?" she asks, filling the silence.

"Going to a party," I tell her. "Some big thing run by the people who own the island. Aunty Desiree bought me a dress and some new shoes."

There is a slight pause on the other end. "That's nice of her," she says, but her voice is stilted like she doesn't think it's nice at all, and now I'm wondering if Omar and Aaron were telling the truth. That maybe Mama has fallen out with Uncle Edmond.

"Well, be good," she says, "Do as you're told and don't cause any trouble."

"I won't, Mama," I promise, but I cross my fingers behind my back when I say it because I know that what I'm about to do, she would definitely think is causing trouble. But if I could explain, I know she would understand why.

There is a knock on the door just as I finish getting ready. Elma pops her head round the door smiling. Her eyes fall on my dress and new shoes. She stands in the doorway, hands on her hips, nodding in approval. I spin round in my dress and the hem flares out as I turn.

"Do you like it?" I ask her.

Elma sighs, nodding her head. "You look wonderful," she says, beaming. "Here, give me your phone."

I pick my phone up from the bed and hand it to her. She points it at me.

"Now give me your best pose." I place a hand on my hip, just like I've seen the models do, and stare at the camera.

Elma chuckles. "Girl, what you doing with your face? Just smile for the camera." I force a smile and she shakes her head. "Smile like yuh seeing your mother, like she is right behind me."

I imagine Mama surprising me, showing up out of the blue because she knows how much I need her. A smile spreads across my lips.

"Beautiful," Elma cries, but my smile fades when I realize Mama isn't here, that she isn't coming. Elma walks across the room and shows me the photos. "You should send them to her," she says. "Now come, everyone is waiting."

I look down at the photos on my phone as she leads me out into the hallway, her hand on my back. "It doesn't look nothing like me," I mumble.

Elma nods in agreement. "You look like one of them," she says patting my back. "Like you belong."

Chapter 12

Mama always told me that my cousins weren't very different to us.

"They just have money, that's all," she would say. "They still cry, and bleed, and hurt, and get sad, just like you and me"

"But what could they have to be sad about," I would say, "when they have all the money in the world?"

She'd look at me with a gentle smile. "Fayson, money only helps to mask your problems, and rich people love to mask their life with shiny things. You remember that when they blind you with sparkles."

I think about this as Aunty Desiree is calling us down the hall, saying we are going to be late. I think about it again when I join them at the front door. Aunty Desiree is wearing a sparkling silver dress that brushes the floor, and Uncle Edmond is wearing a light-blue suit with white shoes. The twins are wearing matching blue suits, the same colour as their dad's and the dress I am wearing.

I think about Mama's words yet again as Aunty Desiree's face lights up when she sees me. It's the first time I have seen her smile so widely. Her hands fly to her mouth, and she stares at me in disbelief.

Uncle Edmond takes me in from head to toe and gives me a short nod of approval.

"Oh, Fayson," Aunty Desiree gasps. "You look just wonderful." I catch Omar chuckling under his hand. I don't know what he's laughing at. I shoot him a glare.

"Shall we go?" Uncle Edmond says, checking his sparkling watch. "Because if you want to make an entrance we need to leave now." He points at his watch. "Right now."

"Okay, okay," Aunty Desiree says. She links arms with me as we leave the house, telling me about the evening and what a wonderful experience it will be for me.

Two men driving two golf carts take us out of my cousins' driveway and back towards the sea.

We pass the jetty where I first arrived and continue round the edge of the Lighthouse Island. Soon after, we turn left down a long sloping driveway that is perfectly lit, with big pillars running along the sides. Trees tower over us like an archway and in the distance I can hear music. I start to feel sick the closer we get, and as we emerge out of the trees, we are confronted by a huge three-storey home lit up like a Christmas tree. The front door is open and two men in red and black uniform greet guests as they arrive.

Everyone is dressed up and I'm relieved that Aunty Desiree bought me these clothes so I don't stand out any more than I already do.

We sit in a line of buggies, each waiting their turn to pull up to the front door. When our turn comes, one of the doormen offers me his hand and helps me out. I follow Aunty Desiree and Uncle Edmond into the house, smoothing down my dress as I go.

A band is playing slow music in the foyer. It's the type of music you hear in old American films where men bow and women curtsy.

The room is filled with men wearing suits and women in sparkly dresses.

A man and a woman approach us with Tia beside them, wearing what looks like a princess dress if she were in a Disney movie. I want to laugh but my awkwardness is more overpowering.

The adults greet each other, and Tia looks me over, bemused. The man standing next to her is taller than everyone else and looks younger too. He turns to me. "And who do we have here?" he says.

"It's the girl I was telling you about, Daddy," Tia says with a smirk. "The one from the city."

"Fayson," Aunty Desiree says proudly, pulling me closer to her. She taps her sparkly white handbag with her manicured fingers. "Her name is Fayson, our niece."

Tia's father smiles broadly. "Ah, the famous Fayson." He offers me his hand. I reluctantly unfold my arms and take it hesitantly.

"I've heard so much about you," he says. "I'm a city man too, you know."

"Not that kind of city, Daddy," Tia interrupts, but he ignores her, still holding on to my hand. "I think we both come from the same place." He winks. Tia's smile fades and I feel myself let out a long breath of relief.

My eyes widen. "You were poor?"

He laughs loudly and his voice echoes around the room, even though the room is full.

"I certainly was. My mother and I lived in the country, in a little hut with one bedroom and a cow called Ms Anne that would stick her head through the window to wake me up."

He laughs again and this time I laugh with him, because that genuinely sounds like a funny thing to happen. He turns to a pouting Tia.

"Why don't you show Fayson around," he suggests, and as I follow Tia down three steps that lead into a large open living room, I can hear him still talking about Ms Anne the cow.

Tia rushes me and my cousins through the house, pointing at rooms uninterestedly and without stopping. "The games room, the TV room, up the stairs are the bedrooms, through there the kitchen and maid quarters, Mama and Daddy's offices, the dining room, the gym." She takes me back into the living room, where the party is, and outside, where floodlights light up a patio. The rest of the gang are all there and I run over to greet them, relieved to see more familiar faces.

Gaby throws her arms round me as though we haven't seen each other in months. She steps back, looking at me.

"You look amazing, Fayson!" she cries. "Doesn't she look amazing, Tia?"

Tia humphs, taking me in from top to bottom. "I wouldn't wear it," she says. The group fall silent.

"She's wearing a dress," Omar says, shrugging. "I don't know what the big deal is." I snap my head to look at him with raised eyebrows, but he doesn't seem to even remember he was just making fun of me.

"Well, it's an honour to be invited to my party," Tia continues. "Even if you didn't get a direct invitation and you used family connections to get here, you should still make an effort. Because if you don't, you might find that you're not allowed to come for the next one." She stares at each person one by one, then turns on her heel and leaves. Gaby pulls me down into a cushioned seat as my heart pounds against my chest.

I lean back against the chair, staring after Tia. "What happens if you stand up to her?"

I say through clenched teeth. The others stare at me in dismay.

"We've told you what would happen," Gaby says, sounding a little annoyed.

"And she just told you," Aaron says, nodding into the house after Tia. "We don't get to come to the island any more."

I look around the group. "So you're just going to let her speak to you like this for ever?" No one answers, but they don't need to. It's obvious they won't do or say anything to upset Tia.

"Forget about her," Gaby says, changing her tone. She turns to face me. "Have you had any more ideas on how to solve the mystery?"

I try to hide the gleeful look on my face.

"You have?" Gaby shouts, beaming.

"Shush," I tell her. "I don't want Tia to hear."

Gaby frowns. "Why?"

I look from her to the others, who are eagerly waiting. "Because I think I may have solved it."

Gaby lets out a shriek, then covers her mouth immediately. The boys move closer.

"Seriously?" Aaron asks.

"You're kidding," says Ace in disbelief.

"No way," Omar adds.

I nod smugly. "But I need proof."

"What kind of proof?" Aaron asks. I glance into the house, where Tia is talking to a group of older girls.

"If I tell you, will you help me?"

They all nod enthusiastically. "And not a word to Tia, not yet."

"Okay…" Gaby says, a little unsure.

Aaron leans forward, catching my eye. "What do we have to do?"

There is a determination in his eyes I haven't seen before.

Chapter 13

When I finish telling everyone the plan, we all quietly tiptoe out to the garden, except for Ace, who enters the house. Aaron leads the way as we crouch against the wall, moving round the side of the house until we reach the front.

When we get there, I poke my head round the wall and spot Ace greeting the doorman, who has his back to us. Ace says something to the doorman and points inside. The doorman goes in, and Ace gives us the thumbs up. The four of us dash across the front yard and down the winding driveway, disappearing into the trees.

When we finally leave Tia's house and reach the road everyone relaxes, and the excited chatter begins. We high-five each other with relief and excitement.

"I can't believe we pulled that off," Aaron says, throwing his head back, face up to the sky.

Gaby grabs me into a tight hug and squeals, "This is so exciting! It's like we're in a movie."

I smile but try not to get excited. "That is just the beginning," I remind them. "We've still got the biggest part to pull off." We follow the road back towards the jetty, then leave the road to follow a footpath between a small sea wall and bushes on the other side.

"Did you check on Ace?" I ask Aaron, as we walk along in a line. He nods.

"He's watching Tia and our parents. Normally they don't ever check on us, but he'll send me a message if anyone gets suspicious."

There is nothing on this side of the island apart from trees and a lone house standing on its own, hidden among the trees and bushes.

It reminds me of those old one-bedroom houses we used to see when we lived in the country. The kind of houses that had a 100-year-old granny living inside. The kind of house Tia's dad talked about.

"Where is he?" I whisper, looking around. Aaron checks his phone. "He'll be doing his rounds. We have maybe ten minutes to get this done. Any longer is too risky."

I nod. "Aaron, why don't you watch the road and signal if you see him. Omar, you wait on the veranda. If you get a signal from Aaron, knock on the door three times."

Aaron nods and stays on the path, while the rest of us walk up to the house. We step on to the porch and up to the front door.

"Am I doing three fast knocks or three slow knocks?" Omar whispers. I notice he's sweating.

"It doesn't matter," I tell him. "Just make sure it's three." He nods, wiping the sweat from his face.

Gaby and I tiptoe to the door and she turns the handle. The door clicks open. Her eyes widen. "He never locks his door," she whispers, delighted that she was right.

This feels wrong, breaking into Thompson's house. Mama would be so angry if she knew what we were doing, but I have to do it if I am going to solve the mystery. This is the only way. I just hope Mama never finds out.

We push the door slightly open and slip through the gap until we are inside.

I turn on my phone light and Gaby does the same as we move around what looks like a small living room not much bigger than the one I have at home.

"I'm so glad I'm doing this with you," Gaby beams, but the light from my phone makes her look like a floating head.

I pass the light over a green flowery sofa, a small TV against the window and a matching chair against the wall. There is a table between the sofa and the TV with a magazine titled *Security Living* and a book titled *How to Be the Best Version of Yourself*.

The house is tidy, with nothing out of place. We leave the living room and enter the kitchen at the back of the house. It's smaller than my kitchen and there's barely enough room for the two of us.

"Here," Gaby hisses, pointing to something on the floor. Under a small table is an old newspaper, and on top of that newspaper are two pairs of boots, both exactly the same.

I lift one of the boots and turn it over to look at the sole. Gaby looks over my shoulder as I open my phone with my other hand and find the photo I took last night. The one upstairs by the window. I stare at the boot then at the photo, for some time.

"It's the same," I say finally.

"I think it is too!" Gaby agrees. "Does that mean you've solved the case?"

I'm about to answer when there is a loud whistle. Seconds later three loud frantic knocks sound on the door. Gaby and I exchange panicked looks and rush into the living room. We open the front door slightly.

"Hurry," Omar hisses from the front yard. I peer to the right and see the caretaker's familiar flashlight moving towards us. I grab Gaby's hand and rush out the door, down the stairs and dive into a bush where the twins are hiding.

Minutes later, the light passes us, with Thompson whistling a tune. We watch through the bush as he climbs the veranda. He stops outside his door, and that's when I notice we forgot to close it behind us.

My heart skips a beat.

He turns to the left, then the right. Then he walks to the edge of his veranda and looks out into the night.

"Oh no," Gaby whispers in my ear. I place a finger to my lips, my eyes not leaving Thompson.

"Who's there?" he calls out. We freeze, barely daring to breathe. He flashes his torch into his front yard and over to the bushes where we are hiding. We duck to the ground as the light passes us. There is silence, and I peer through a gap in the bushes to see him enter his house and close the door.

"Run!" I hiss. The others don't need to be told twice, as we all scramble out the bush and race at top speed away from Thompson's house.

We only slow down when we reach Tia's house, where we stop to take a breath. It's only then we realize how close we came to being caught, and start laughing.

As we head down the driveway, Omar goes into a long story about how frightening it was waiting on that veranda. "I've never been so scared in my life," he says holding his chest, "and when my brother whistled, I thought I was going to have a heart attack!"

I slow down as we near the house. "Guys…"

They turn to look at me, then at what I have in my hand.

I hold one of Thompson's boots out in front of me. "How am I going to hide this?"

Ace meets us at the front door.

"How did it go?" he asks, looking hopeful.

Omar groans. "Fayson stole Thompson's boot."

Ace looks at him blankly, then at me. His eyes widen. "You did what?"

We stand outside the front door. "How else am I going to prove my case?" I tell them. "A detective solves the case with facts, and you all know that Tia will call me a liar—but she can't call me a liar if the boot is right in front of her."

The twins shake their heads in dismay, and even Gaby smiles painfully at me. "It sort of, maybe… might get us in trouble?" she suggests.

I sigh. "Well, I can't take it back."

"You can't take it in there either!" Omar has snapped back to his usual annoying self. "I think they're going to notice you carrying a boot in your hand."

I flash him a sarcastic smile. "You think?…"

"Wait here," Aaron says. He walks over to where the golf carts are parked under a large coconut tree, and approaches one of the drivers. The driver looks over at us then back at Aaron. Seconds later the driver gets into the golf cart and Aaron calls us over.

We rush over and pile on to the nearest golf cart.

"What did you tell him?" I whisper to Aaron.

He shrugs. "That I needed to go home."

I stare at him. "That's it?"

He chuckles at my expression. "Yes, that's it."

I settle in with him and Gaby on either side of me, Omar and Ace behind. Just as we pull away, someone jumps out in front of the cart, forcing the driver to stop abruptly.

"Where are you going, without me?"

Tia. My heart sinks. She jumps on the back of the cart, next to Ace and Omar.

"Where are we going?" she repeats, as the cart takes off down the driveway. "I just need to change my shoes, my feet are sore," I tell her. I feel Gaby's eyes on me as I slowly lower the boot to the floor.

The short drive back to the twins' house is excruciating. Tia moans the whole way, saying she should have stayed at her house, where it was much more interesting.

"I can walk back with you if you like?" I hear Ace suggest.

"Well, I'm here now," she snaps. "But you better be quick, Fayson. Daddy's making an announcement and I think he might have bought me a puppy. I don't want to miss it."

I lift the boot off the floor of the golf cart and nod, as the night wind blows through my hair. "I won't make you miss it," I promise her. "I'll be super quick."

"You better be," she snaps.

As soon as the driver stops the cart outside the twins' house, Elma opens the front door, much to my relief. She must have heard us coming. I jump out of the cart shouting, "Wait there, I'll be right back!" With the boot held in front of me, hidden from Tia's gaze, I run inside the house, through the living room, along the corridor and to my bedroom.

Inside the room I hide the boot inside the wardrobe, behind my pack. When I return, everyone except Tia looks at me quizzically. I give the others a tiny nod and relief floods their faces.

I wake up the next morning to Elma the maid opening my curtains and sunlight streaming in.

"Good morning, Ms Fayson," she says in her usual cheery voice.

I shield my eyes from the bright sun, desperately wanting to go back to sleep. I went to bed last night missing Mama. After the party, I tried to call her, knowing she was at work and wouldn't answer, but that didn't make it any easier. I left a message, hoping she would call me back.

"Breakfast will be ready in five minutes," Elma says, before leaving and closing the door. I roll on to my back, wiping the sleep from my eyes. Today is the day I reveal who the shadow is… but instead of feeling excited I feel homesick. Maybe it was seeing everyone from the group with their families that made me feel left out. Although the twins are family, we are so different it never feels that way.

185

When I finally get to breakfast the whole family is there, which is unusual because we rarely eat with Uncle Edmond. I tense when I see him sitting at the head of the table. Something about Uncle Edmond doesn't make me feel relaxed at all.

I pull out my usual chair next to Aaron and sit down.

"Good morning, Fayson," Aunty Desiree says from the other end of the table. I avoid her eyes, which I know are fixed on me.

"Good morning, Aunty, good morning, Uncle."

I pour myself a glass of orange juice and wait for him to correct my speech. Instead, Uncle Edmond talks about the garden needing trimming and how they should call Desmond the gardener to come and tidy it up. They both look out to the garden, which you can see clearly from the table, and a faint line of the sea though the trees in the

186

distance. The folding glass doors are open and a faint breeze wafts in.

"So, you ready?" Aaron whispers.

I take a deep breath and nod. "Yes, I'm ready."

He grins widely. "I knew you could do it, Fayson."

I feel a rush of warmth that I have made my cousins proud.

Omar frowns at us from across the table, then picks his plate up and brings it to the other side so that he is next to us.

"What are you whispering about?" he says, sitting down and making a clatter as he does. "Are you talking about the meeting? About the shadow?"

Aaron tells him to shush, as their father glares at them. We continue to eat in silence, only the noise of our knives and forks making any sound in the otherwise silent table. Uncle Edmond hasn't asked me anything and Aunty Desiree isn't her usual talkative self. The room feels heavy, like when Mama is upset with me but isn't ready to tell me why.

Uncle Edmond finishes his breakfast first, wipes his mouth with a napkin and leans forward, his elbows on the table. I feel his eyes on me and my heart quickens its pace.

"Fayson," he says finally. "We should talk about last night, don't you think?"

I look up from my plate, my heart quickening.

Chapter 14

"I thought we were doing a good thing bringing you here," Aunty Desiree says. "When the boys suggested it, we agreed it would be a nice break for you and your mother."

I look at them both, wondering what she's talking about.

Aunty Desiree glances across the table to Uncle Edmond. "Didn't we, Edmond?"

He sighs. "Yes, I can't always help my sister the way she wants me to, but we thought this would be a nice gesture for you both."

I look to the boys for some help, but they seem as confused as I am.

"But we seem to have got it wrong," Aunty Desiree continues. "When Tia told us you went off last night without telling us, we were very disappointed."

I sit back into my chair with a heavy sigh, folding my arms across my chest. Of course it was Tia.

"She didn't do it, Mama," Aaron interrupts. "It was me."

Aunty Desiree raises her hand. "Don't worry, your time will come." Her voice is so low and seething with emotion that Aaron doesn't say another word.

They look at me and wait for an answer. I feel the twins' eyes glancing up under their eyelashes.

"I never ask to be here," I say finally, my lips pouting and my breathing fast. "Is you that bring me here."

"*I didn't ask to be here,*" Uncle Edmond corrects me. I push my chair back so hard it wobbles from side to side.

"Mi never ask to be here," I repeat. "I like my house, and I like my life, and I like my mother, and I like how I speak. I don't like all dis pretend, pretend, dress up, dress up, fake things, because I don't know what is real. I don't know if yuh even like me because nothing is real here. Nobody here is real!" I scream.

I spin on my heels and storm out of the dining room. My feet start to run, and I rush into my room and close the door behind me, throwing myself on the bed and crying my eyes out.

When Aaron and Omar open the door, I am already packing my things, my face stained with tears.

"What are you doing?" Aaron asks, sitting on the edge of the bed while I throw what little I have into my bag. I wipe my face with the back of my hand.

"They're not going to want me to stay now," I tell them through sniffs. "They probably already called Mama and told her what I did. I'll be on the next boat back to the main island in the next hour, you watch."

Omar sits down on my bed next to his brother. "Fayson, please don't go," he pleads. "It won't be the same without you. Plus, you still haven't revealed who the shadow is."

I throw the last book into my pack and zip it, then hang my head. "I don't want to disappoint Mama," I whisper, sniffing away the tears. My heart feels so heavy it hurts.

"Fayson." I look up and Aunty Desiree and Uncle Edmond are standing in the doorway. "Fayson, what are you doing?" she says, walking into the room.

"She's packing," Omar says. "She thinks you want to send her home."

Aunty gets on the floor in front of me and takes my reluctant hands. "We want you here," she says gently. "Of course we want you here. And despite what you think, you made quite an impression on the Brookes. Tia's father adores you. In fact, he said Tia could learn a few things from you."

She lets go of my hands and wipes my tears away. "We do have rules though, and if you're part of this family you have to abide by them."

I sniff back the tears. "What are the rules?"

"Well, no storming from the table and no raising your voice," she says.

"And no Patwah?" I ask.

She glances up at Uncle Edmond, who is now sitting on the edge of the bed next to the twins. He chuckles, shaking his head.

"Boy, you have your mother's stubbornness that's for sure." He crosses his legs and uncrosses them. "Listen, this is a different world, and I've seen both sides. No one understands Patwah here, and those that do make judgements. I've had to learn the hard way, that to be accepted, you have to adjust. I'm helping you so you don't experience what I did."

I think about this for some time. Uncle Edmond makes it sound like he's doing a good thing, helping me, but it doesn't feel like he's helping me. It still doesn't sound right, but I don't know if that's because I'm not like them, so maybe I just don't understand how their world works.

Aunty Desiree strokes my face and beams at me when I look at her. "This is a great place with wonderful opportunities," she says. "The friends you make here could change your life. Just let us know where you're going. This is a small island but bad things can happen even on tiny islands."

I don't answer, because my heart still feels heavy and nothing they're saying is making me feel any better.

"Now unpack your things," Aunty Desiree says, getting to her feet with a groan and saying she's too old to sit on the floor like that. As they both leave, I call after them.

"Uncle Edmond..."

He turns. "Yes?"

"Do you speak Patwah?"

His face changes and he becomes solemn. "I used to speak it all the time with your mother," he says, "back when she would call me. Now I don't have much reason to." He turns and leaves as Aunty Desiree wraps her arm round him.

Omar runs to the door and peers round the corner. "They're gone," he announces. The twins both look at me in anticipation.

"You ready?"

I sigh, staring at my packed bag. "Sure, why not. I'm ready."

We head out into the garden. I carry the boot in a carrier bag, and the twins walk either side of me, giving me words of encouragement.

"You've got this," Omar says, patting me on the back.

"We knew you would solve it, Fayson," Aaron adds, and gives me a reassuring smile.

When we reach the hut, nestled among the trees, Aaron does his secret knock: three knocks together, pause, three knocks, pause, two knocks, pause, one knock. I don't understand the sequence or why they chose that, but my mind is too full of other things to worry about their secret knocks.

In fact, I feel a little sick.

The door opens and Gaby looks out. She beams when she sees me and gives me a secret thumbs up before opening the door to let us in.

Inside, the room has changed. Tia is still behind her desk, but everyone else is sitting on chairs that look very much like the chairs round the twins' dining table. There is a space between the chairs, which I use to approach Tia's desk while the others settle down.

I place the bag on the floor in front of me and take a deep breath before connecting eyes with Tia.

There is a confident smirk on her face as she sits for a few minutes, just staring at me. It's only when a timer goes off does she sit up and press stop on her phone. She leans on her desk and her smirk grows bigger.

"So, it's officially seventy-two hours since you first took on the challenge to find the shadow," she says. "And now, your time is up." Tia looks at me as if waiting for me to respond, but I don't know what she expects me to say.

"Okay..." I say, shrugging, "I mean, that's why we're here."

Her smirk turns sour. "So now you can admit it. You failed. You can go back to wherever you came from." She pauses to think. "Where was it again? The shopping centre?" She laughs.

I take a long deep breath. "Can I start now?" I say impatiently.

Her smile wavers. "Start?"

I nod, bending over and taking Thompson's boot out of the bag. "Yes," I say, watching her face fall. "Can I start?"

She leans back in her chair, raising her eyebrows. "Go on."

I stand the boot on her desk, so it blocks out most of her face, forcing her to tilt her head to one side to see me.

"The first thing I thought of when you showed me the shadow, was the same question many detectives ask themselves," I begin, standing to the left of the desk and facing the group. "Is this person real, and if they are what do they want?

"The next thing is to visit the place of the crime. You will remember that me, Aaron and Omar went first, and we heard a sound but by the time we made it upstairs there was no one there. We assumed it was the wind, but if it wasn't the wind, and was a person, this meant the person, or ghost, was quick. Possibly young—so that ruled out almost every adult on this island."

I pace in front of the desk as I start to get into it, as though I have been doing this my whole life. As though a camera is in the corner of the room filming my final big scene.

"Then I suggested we all sleep there. Maybe I or the twins were too slow, but

I was sure the shadow couldn't outrun all of us. So we slept there, and as you all know someone did come, but for some reason, the shadow escaped all six of us. But they left one clue."

I pick up the boot and show them. "A footprint."

Tia groans, rolling her eyes. "We've already been over this. Thompson showed us that we ruined the scene with all our footsteps. Is that all you've got?"

I turn to her. "You're right, he did. But then I noticed one footprint completely different from all the rest. It stood out because it was bigger and almost swallowed all the others. I thought it must be Thompson's footprints from when you'd brought him in, so I went upstairs to the room at the top, because I knew there was one place we hadn't stepped. One place Thompson hadn't been."

Everyone sits forward, even Tia.

"When I looked, there was only one set of footprints by the window, which could only have been the shadow's."

I take my phone out of my pocket and show them the photo of the footprint.

"Two footprints on their own by the window… matching the same footprints downstairs." I show the bottom of Thompson's boots. "The same footprint I saw up and down the road on my first day here." I turn to Tia. "So how did you get Thompson there so quick?"

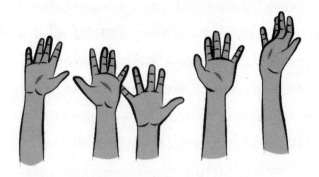

Chapter 15

Everyone joins me in looking at Tia. She sits forward, completely unimpressed. "Thompson patrols the island. It's his job."

I nod, as if buying it. "So he just happened to be outside at the same time you went to get him?"

The group starts to murmur, as I haven't revealed this part to them. They look at each other, confused.

Aaron asks what everyone is thinking: "Are you saying Tia had something to do with it?"

"I don't know what she's saying, but she's wrong," Tia retorts. "First of all, that boot you have in your hand? It was a present from my father. He likes to hike and wanted Thompson to have a good pair of boots to do his rounds in. My father has the same pair. Secondly, don't you remember how on the first night you came, I showed you Thompson doing his rounds at the exact time the shadow was flashing the light?"

She sits back triumphantly. My chest falls. She's right. I hadn't thought of that. I glance at Gaby, who seems as disappointed as me.

"Just as I thought then," Tia says. "You haven't solved anything, and—" she glares at the twins—"that's what happens when you bring in weirdos from shopping malls."

"She's not a weirdo, she's our cousin," Omar growls back at her.

"Well, that makes sense," Tia snaps back.

I stare at the boot as they argue back and forth. I was so sure I had that right. I run it through my head again: the shadow, the flashing light, the footprints, the person running down the winding stairs.

"So, you can leave now," Tia says, turning her attention back to me. "You don't get to be part of our club." She points to the door. I stare at the boot, then at her, and my heart skips a beat.

"Your father," I blurt out, and it all clicks as soon as I say it. Her face confirms it. "It was your father. You told me the day you met me that he likes to play games with you. That you would trick people all the time and it was your favourite game to see how long it took people to guess."

I watch her smile disappear.

"The footprint wasn't Thompson's, it was your father—he was playing your game, for you." The words start spilling out so fast

I barely have time to take a breath. "It would explain why you showed us Thompson that first night, to trick me. And you told Thompson to come to the lighthouse that night, because when I woke up you were texting someone, and not long after, the shadow appeared. It was why you made a noise to warn them. You didn't want me to solve it! You wanted me to fail."

"That's why you didn't want us bringing anyone in to help us solve it," Aaron adds, sitting forward. "You wanted it to be just us, because you didn't want anyone to figure it out, you wanted to trick us."

"Like we're you're toys or something," Omar adds.

"That makes sense," Ace says, nodding. "You told me that you knew Fayson would fail, and I didn't understand how you knew that."

We all look to Tia. I wait for her to deny it. To say I'm just a sore loser. She groans, throwing her hands up in the air. "Well, it was only supposed to be fun, but then you brought her into it."

"But I was scared," Gaby says. "I told you that if it was one of your pranks you should tell me, and you said it wasn't."

Tia rolls her eyes. "Well that's because you're gullible, Gaby, and besides, I didn't want anyone to get my prize."

I frown. "What prize?"

She sighs. "Daddy said whoever figures it out gets a prize, but if no one figures it out, I get it."

Silence falls among the group.

"There's a prize?" Omar shouts in disbelief.

Tia shrugs. "It doesn't matter anyway; I still vote you out. You guessed it wrong first time and so my decision is the same." She sneers at me. "You're not one of us."

"No, I'm not," I agree, and turn to leave. I walk past the group and towards the door.

"We're voting you out as leader," Gaby blurts out to Tia.

I turn to see Tia jumping to her feet. "You can't vote me out!" she screams, stamping her foot.

Aaron gets to his feet as well. "Yes she can. It's in the rules, if the majority of us agree… and I vote you out too." Aaron looks around the room.

Omar jumps up, almost knocking his chair over. "Me too," he says, "because you're mean, and didn't tell us there was a prize. Plus you called my cousin names and only I can do that, not you."

A smile pulls at the corner of my lips.

Ace stands and lowers his head. "I'm sorry, Tia, but it's not working out for me either. I don't think you should lead our gang any more."

"That's four of us," Aaron says, his voice shaky.

Tia's face turns to thunder. "You can't vote me out, it's my island." She screams.

"You can still be friends with us," Gaby says nervously.

Tia throws daggers at Gaby. "Do you want me to tell my father? Do you want me to make him throw you off this island for ever? I can and I will."

When no one answers, she throws back her chair and storms over to the door, pushing me out of the way. Then she yanks the door open and storms out, screaming, "You're going to regret this!"

The group look at each other frantically.

"Will she do it?" Gaby asks.

"My parents love this island," Ace says. "Maybe we should let her stay?"

I watch as they crumble at the thought of the island being taken away from them all because Tia is not getting her own way. It makes me see red.

I run out the door and the others follow me.

"Fayson, where are you going?" Gaby calls after me.

"I'm going to talk to her father myself," I shout and pick up speed.

"They're having a grown-up brunch thing," Gaby calls after me. "We're not allowed."

I ignore her, chasing after Tia as she disappears down the twins' driveway. I have nothing left to lose. I've already upset Aunty Desiree and Uncle Edmond. How much more upset could they be? They could send me home, but I want to go home. I hate it here.

By the time I get to Tia's house, she is nowhere to be seen. I knock on the front door but no one answers, so I run round the side of the house the same way we did last night. As I round the corner, I hear laughter and voices.

Six or seven tables are set up by the pool, with grown-ups sitting around them. The tables are filled with food and drinks. Tia's parents sit at a table at the top end of the pool, and I can see Tia rushing through the tables towards her father.

I sprint over to the pool, but she has already reached her father, who wraps his arms round her.

Aunty Desiree and Uncle Edmond spot me on the other side of the pool.

"Fayson?" he calls over.

I ignore them and run along the opposite side.

"Mr Brookes, sir," I call, out of breath. Tia glares at me but I ignore her.

"Fayson!" he says, with a raise of his eyebrows. "What brings you children here? You know this is a grown-up event."

"I know, Daddy," she says, pouting, "but—"

"I figured out the case," I blurt out, before Tia can get another word in.

He turns in his seat.

"The case you and your daughter planned, with the shadow? She didn't want me to solve it because she wanted the prize for herself, but…" I hear stirring around the tables and look behind me to see the rest of the gang just arriving. The adults are not happy, so I talk quickly.

"She didn't tell anyone there was a prize," I shout. Tia's father turns his head to look at her and she lowers her eyes. "But I figured it out, even without knowing there was a prize, and the group helped me."

He lets go of his daughter and turns completely to face me. "And what was it you figured out, Fayson?"

I take a breath. "That you would do anything for Tia, so you pretended to be the shadow. She said you've been playing these games with her since she was young, but I don't think you know she has been doing it knowing that it scares some of her friends.

"But maybe you did know and love her so much that you do it anyway, even though it is wrong. I think my Mama would do almost anything for me, but she wouldn't let me hurt anyone. She wouldn't do this if she knew that when someone figured it out, the person who started it all would threaten to have everyone removed from the island and keep the prize for herself." I take a deep breath, realizing I am trembling. "I don't think anyone good would let that happen, not when the case was solved fair and square."

Silence falls all around us, and for a minute I think everyone may have frozen. Or maybe I'm asleep and I dreamt this all.

He glowers at Tia. "Is that true?"

Tia sits opposite her father with pleading eyes. "Daddy, they're trying to vote me out of the group. I don't want them here any more. I want new friends." He glares at her in disbelief, and looks to his wife as if to check he has heard right. Her mother shakes her head.

"Tia," she says in dismay.

Mr Brookes looks around him, embarrassed, then turns his gaze back to me. He forces a smile. "Congratulations, Fayson. The prize is in fact an electric scooter. I'll have it delivered to your uncle's house later on."

I shake my head. "I don't need the prize, sir. I'll be leaving soon. I just don't want you to kick the others off the island."

He laughs a short laugh. "No one is getting kicked off Lighthouse Island," he says. "The people you see in front of us are our friends. We hold each of them dear to our hearts. We thought their children would be a great influence on Tia." He shakes his head in disappointment.

"We still want Tia in the group," Gaby says from behind me.

"But we want a different leader," Aaron adds.

Her father smiles. "You are too kind, and she accepts." Tia starts to protest, but he ignores her. "Hopefully your kindness will rub off on my daughter."

I glance at Tia, whose head is hanging low and her shoulders bent forward. Satisfied that the others are safe, I turn and walk away.

"Mama," I say down the phone.

I have locked myself in the bathroom because I was afraid someone would disturb me. There is no privacy in this house, even though it's huge.

"Fayson, everything okay?" I didn't expect her to answer as she's usually at work at this

time, but when she does I am so relieved
I nearly cry.

"Mama, thank you for not being rich,"
I tell her down the phone.

She laughs. "What?"

"I've seen rich people, Mama, and they
are not happy, not the way we are. I know
I was mad because you couldn't come here,
but I think it's better you didn't because you
would have been so mad at them. Mama,
they're nothing like us."

There is a pause on the other end, and
I think she may have been cut off.

"Mama? You there?"

"Fayson, everyone has problems," she
says quietly. "Money doesn't change that.
Sometimes it changes people, sometimes it
pulls people apart."

I lean against the wall, staring at the
ceiling, and I want to ask her if she means
Uncle Edmond—if money pulled them

apart—but it's enough just to hear her voice.

"Sometimes, Fayson, you are the richest person in the room, even if you have no money," she whispers. "Maybe you can teach them about that. About your richness. You have so much of it. You have so much to show them. Things money can't buy."

I sit on the tiled floor thinking about what she said, long after the call has ended.

When I step outside, everyone is sitting on the main patio outside the living room, on the wicker chairs. Gaby waves at me and I join them, finding a seat.

"Well, that was intense," Omar jokes, swinging his legs back and forth against the chair.

"I don't think I've ever seen Tia so…" Gaby searches for a word.

"Sad?" I finish off for her. She nods, smiling weakly.

Aaron sits forward in his chair and glances over at me. "So, we were thinking about someone new to lead the group," he says. "We had a vote while you were gone. Sorry."

I'm surprised how hurt I feel that they voted without me, even though I'm not really part of the gang. I'm only here for a few weeks.

"The voting was unanimous," he continues. "We voted for you."

I blink at them in disbelief. Did I hear right?

Gaby beams and rushes over, throwing her arms round me. "I told you," she whispers. "I told you from the minute I saw you. I knew!"

"But," I stammer, "I'm only here for a few weeks."

Aaron raises his eyebrows. "You don't want to come back?"

Gaby nudges me playfully.

"Think of all the adventures we can have," says Aaron.

"The cases still to uncover," Ace adds.

"The shirts you can throw up on!" Omar pipes up, and he starts to laugh. I look at them all, waiting for me to answer.

Gaby nudges me again. "Well? What do you say?"

I think about what it would be like to come here every holiday. To have them as my friends. And about Mama, and the things we could do together on her time off that I would miss. I think about my dream to be a detective and how it came true. Lastly I think about the lighthouse, the shadow and the hut hidden at the end of the garden.

There is only one answer. So I tell them, knowing my decision will change everything.

"Well, I suppose you do need me," I say, "and Mama will be working most days."

"We don't *need* you," Omar says, but his brother shoots him a look. Omar sighs. "Okay, we do need you a little bit, I suppose."

"And we can make it official," Gaby says eagerly. "We can be a proper detective agency, solving all the mysteries on the island."

"It's definitely better than just meeting in the hut for no reason," Aaron agrees, nodding.

"The name has to change though," I tell them. "A real detective agency always has a good name." Everyone starts to think of a name, their eyebrows squeezed together deep in thought.

"The Island Crew?" Ace suggests. We all look at him as we roll the name around in our heads.

"Di Island Crew," I say. "Di, not The." Omar and Aaron smile a knowing smile at me.

Gaby nods in approval. "Di Island Crew… I like it."

"So does that mean you're coming back?" Aaron asks.

I feel their eyes on me, waiting. "Yes," I say finally. "If we're going to solve mysteries, then I'm coming back." Before I can even finish, they all rush me, throwing themselves on me.

"On three," Aaron says, laying his hand out. We all pile our hands on top of each other, making a pyramid.

"Di Island Crew!" we cheer, and my heart sings knowing this is the beginning of my dream.

No more pretending to be an FBI agent. This is real.

Me, Fayson Dawson, the girl from the city, who lives in an apartment with only her Mama and her book friends.

I am officially a real-life detective.

Wait until I tell Mama about this.

Next time,
Di Island Crew investigates...

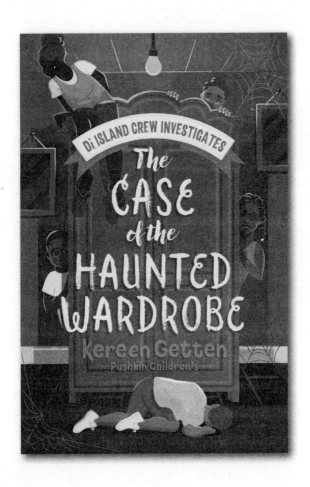

Di ISLAND CREW INVESTIGATES

The
CASE
of the
HAUNTED
WARDROBE

Kereen Getten
Pushkin Children's

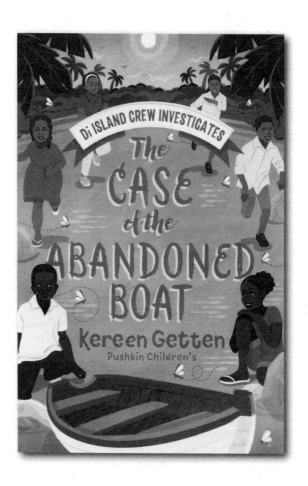

Di ISLAND CREW INVESTIGATES

The
CASE
of the
ABANDONED
BOAT

Kereen Getten

Pushkin Children's